The Queen of Jasmine Country

Sharanya Manivannan is the author of the short-story collection *The High Priestess Never Marries*, which won the 2015-16 South Asia Laadli Media and Advertising Award for Gender Sensitivity (Best Book – Fiction) and was shortlisted for the TATA Lit Live! First Book Award (Fiction) and longlisted for the Atta Galatta – Bangalore Literature Festival Book Prize. She is also the author of two books of poetry, *Witchcraft* and *The Altar of the Only World*, and a picture book for children, *The Ammuchi Puchi*.

The Queen of Jasmine Country is her first novel.

Books by Sharanya Manivannan

Witchcraft

The Ammuchi Puchi

The High Priestess Never Marries

The Altar of the Only World

The Queen of Jasmine Country

Sharanya Manivannan

HarperCollins *Publishers* India

First published in hardback in India by
HarperCollins *Publishers* in 2018

HarperCollins Publishers India, Cyber City, Building 10-A, Gurugram,
Haryana-122002, India
www.harpercollins.co.in

2 4 6 8 10 9 7 5 3 1

P-ISBN: 978-93-5302-384-3
E-ISBN: 978-93-5302-385-0

Typeset in 11/14 Sabon LT Std at
Manipal Digital Systems, Manipal

Printed and bound at
MicroPrints India, New Delhi

MIX
Paper
FSC FSC™ C218906

This product is made of FSC®-certified and other controlled material.

HarperCollins Publishers, Macken House, 39/40 Mayor Street
Upper, Dublin 1, D01 C9W8, Ireland

For Amma and Appa

850CE
Puduvai
near Madurai, Tamilagam

It was not always there, and one day it was.

My body was used to blood, its monthly spillage, but my nature was not. Its surge rendered my body a conch, keeper of a riptide. Desire – this new language – spun me on itself like a discus.

At night, I walk as deep into the groves as I can go without being sighted, my anklets unclasped and held in my fist. Metal protects against malevolence, especially of the unseen kind. I turn circles, unable to sleep because of the bird in my throat and the blood drumming in every place where my pulse can be felt. I pluck wild hibiscus and golden magnolia, its petals luminously white under starlight. I lay myself upon red ochre earth and entangle my limbs and hair in grass and tender tulasi. I seep into the earth, its touch and mine the same, and then I blossom.

Maybe everywhere there are those like me – people who smoulder sun-like but singe as easily as feathers. But I know of no one else who is fevered by a secret so large. Bolstered by the sleeping women of my family, I wake up drenched in sweat and tears. The night is as dark and still as a vessel of unstirred indigo. I sit up, still trembling, and crouch over to unfasten my silver-belled anklets, then carefully raise myself from the floor. I adjust my loosely draped sari over my body, and slip from the boundaries of home. And then, I run. Past the well with its dismemberments of moonlight. Past the cowshed, where no creature betrays me. And then beyond, burning, into the grove where I came from. Into the grove where the parrots know not to mimic the sounds of my ecstasy and the undergrowth will not keep the shape of my trespass – and my body, this roaring, returns to and becomes earth and fire, and floods lush, and flowers.

1

Perhaps this was what happened on my first night on earth.

Perhaps it wasn't the very first night. Perhaps there were a few nights before it, when a woman had held me to her breasts and fed me, their weight easing along with my hunger. Perhaps we looked into one another's eyes. Perhaps she gave me a name that only the winds know now, a name I would not know myself by if she were ever to call me at a marketplace, if she turned away from a procession and ran in my direction, if she emerged from the shadows under a banyan tree one lonesome afternoon and laid her claim to me. With or without having bestowed upon me a name, I would like to think that she would always know me.

Perhaps this was what happened then, on one of those earliest nights of my life. I woke a few moments after I was laid quietly on the ground in this tulasi grove, when the wetness of the earth had seeped slightly into the cloth I had been bound in. I saw stars when I opened my eyes. They would always be there, in all the years to come when I would seek them, as I aged almost nothing in contrast.

I was born in the season of mid-summer monsoon, under the constellation of the lion, and then I was abandoned.

Here's what I can never prove: that on the night the tulasi grove first embraced me, a man knelt to lay me on the ground carefully and smoothed droplets of rain from my forehead. That his teeth were white but he kept his mouth closed. That he moved as quickly as he could and merged into the trees, his anklets faintly chiming, muffled by the rustle of grass. And then he disappeared. No, surely he waited to see what he knew would happen. Perhaps I only truly know this: that, somewhere beyond all certainty of belonging, I will never stop looking for the blue-black of his skin, and for the taste of the milk that was still on my breath.

I opened my mouth and wailed.

'A baby!' the voice of the woman who was not yet my mother exclaimed. But her husband was already running, the plantain leaf of food before him forgotten.

This is what I believe happened, in the minutes before my parents made me theirs. And these things I know to be true, for they told me later: how my mother did not ponder till afterwards how she could have known that I was alone, that I was neither a traveller's child nor a neighbour's. How she had placed a vessel of cow's milk on the fire the moment her husband's back disappeared into the shadows and then thrown it out, suddenly afraid it had curdled since the morning. How my father – fearing what? – had rushed into the grove on pure instinct, not a word exchanged between them first.

And later still, as I watched him, I learned: what my father had feared were birds of prey, the curiosity of insects, the creatures of the wild that he loved and so understood to not always be loving in return. My father knew he was my father even before he knew me. He ran into his grove of tulasi barefoot, kernels of cooked millet still wedged in his fingernails, and lifted me into his arms. He saw my face by starlight and by a moon as shy as the secret of my origin.

And he carried me back, very slowly, through the paths his footsteps had patterned over years, past the dark shapes of the plants he raised. My mother had lit a lantern and waited by the entrance that opened onto the garden. This too would become familiar to me – her waiting at the end of days that lingered long after nightfall, the light by which she showed us the way.

Now, I move constantly under cover of darkness and commit acts of subterfuge like the daughter of a thief. I surrender to the carnal like the daughter of a dancer. I scatter enigmas like the daughter of a shell-reader. I swallow the ocean in my dreams like the daughter of a diver.

And still, I smell of wild jasmine and tender basil like the daughter of a gardener, my fingertips tinged with turmeric like the daughter of a woman whose world is the hearth – and this is who I am.

In the year following the night when I was discovered in the grove, our king would annex the north of the island shaped like a mango. On my first birthday, my father would allow me to taste jaggery, which sweetened the offering at his favourite temple. The harvest would be rich that year, and for the sake of their child, my parents would replace the blue cactus on the periphery of the fields with thickets of sugarcane. Everywhere, a sweetness. My mother's songs as dense as honey, my father's poems as translucent. In the far north-east of the world, honey mixed with saltpetre, realgar and sulphur created a smoking powder that could burn a house down – but it was not, as the alchemists desired, the elixir of life. In the far north-west of the world, a ship made of oak was buried with the remains of two women – a queen and her daughter, or a shaman and her handmaiden, or some other configuration of loyalty or love that will come to be forgotten – and with them were placed tapestries, enamelled objects, and several animals that drew their last breaths inside that ark. And in this small new town under the flag of the double fish, in the deep south of a bejewelled peninsula, Arali and her husband, Vishnuchittan, found themselves sometimes forgetting all else that they were before they became the guardians of a baby girl found amongst leaves still glossy with recent rain.

Sixteen-and-a-half years have passed in the embrace of this garden. My father can no longer lift me onto his shoulders so that I can see above any crowd, but I hold what he showed me just as true as I hold the stars I first saw on my back that long-ago night. I raised, and raise still, my gaze beyond the certain to see through all of time, past the delusion of bondage, into the truth of all things.

And this is why, on some mornings after I have lost count of the hours as they betrayed me, he does not ask me where I have spent the night. I catch him looking into the distance as though the first birdsong has something to teach him. And if he catches me, breathlessly making my way back through the bramble that protects the grove, he neither speaks nor sways. But still I blush like the sky as it dawns. For my father is always listening.

I grew along with the fence of sugarcane. My teeth, when they came in, grew strong on the flesh of those stalks. I never wondered why my parents did not protect me with a deceit of love, for it was very little time before I became incapable of accepting a lie. And besides, that memory never left me, of those two bright stars above me in the night. The scent of recent rain still calls to that place in me that knows it was abandonment that brought me a home.

'Kodhai,' my father would say as I worked alongside him in his garden, learning how to turn decay into nourishment and to recognize not-yet-bloomed flowering plants by their leaves. 'Whoever brought you to me had no fear of being refused. This is why I sometimes think an emissary of Raja Srimara Srivallabha must have been the one. The king knew that there was no child in our house. After all, the first time I was in his court, he had promised me a life of fullness for as long as he or his descendants remain on the throne.'

My grandmother, Padmamma, was more imaginative. 'You must have been the child of a buffalo!' she would groan, pulling my frizzy curls into plaits, or pouring a vessel of water over my head as I ran naked from her slippery grip, or forcing balls of food into my mouth. 'A buffalo and a woman who wandered singing, clad only by the sky,' she would mutter in resignation, wiping coconut oil, or water, or spilt food from her hands.

For as long as he lived, my grandfather, Mukunda Acharya, believed I did not have human lineage. He was convinced that I had manifested birthless amongst the tulasi in the absence of womb sac or womanly labour. His theory was taken very lightly in our home, even if nothing was ever said to his face. If I fidgeted in a queue at a temple, my mother would pinch me and hiss, 'Do you see anyone offering you flowers or chanting your name? Do you see anyone asking you for a boon? You're a little girl misbehaving, nothing more.' But Mukunda Acharya traced his devotion, or at least its erudition, back six generations. And because that made me the eighth in his lineage, even if I was a girl, he told me each day about the eighth incarnation of his supreme lord, Maha Vishnu – the tricky and iridescent Krishna, who wears a peacock feather tucked into his crown. And even if they had wanted to, nothing my parents or grandmother could say would refute the spell these stories held me under. I woke with a name of Vishnu on my breath; when I chewed, a name of Vishnu was in my saliva; and now, sometimes in the garden at midnight it is a name of Vishnu that escapes my lips in bliss. And so that I could speak this name aloud as often as I could, Vishnuchittan permitted me to call him by his name, and not as Appa or Iyah as was correct.

My mother, Arali, refused such impudence. She who fed me with cow's milk, envying the creature that could give me what she could not, would only be Amma.

It was Amma's tale that I loved the most. 'Because my belly could not hold a baby, the garden absorbed my tears. The garden is my heart. That's where you were born.' And then, when I started to cry, moved by what she said even though I could not completely understand it, she would laugh and say, 'I bought you from a trader of pearls from Korkai. I had only a bagful of tamarind to exchange with, because your ruthless father had already replaced all the crops with tulasi. If I had had two bags, I would have been able to get a pearl instead. And instead of your arms around my neck, I'd wear a thread with that pearl!'

'You would never.'

'I would!'

'No!'

One day I went too far. Unable to bear this play, I shouted, 'Then give me back to my real mother!' And Amma's face shrivelled like stroked mimosa leaves. I fled into the grove and waited there until Padmamma found me, crying over the bodies of vermillion ladybugs I had squashed in my rage.

Now, in the long nights, I sometimes find them crawling on my body. And I wonder what it would be like to paint my lips with their colour, like the troupe of dancers who passed through Puduvai one Pongal when I was a child, who threw and caught each other in impossible leaps and contortions. But mostly I just watch them as they run over my skin, their tiny feet grazing my goosebumps. They are not what a lover's fingers must be like… But when will I know?

Vishnuchittan began to teach me how to read before his father could stop him. And even before that, when I had barely begun to speak, he sat me on his lap with a tray of uncooked rice before me, and pressed my finger into the grain to curve and line the letter அ, the first letter of the alphabet. I made a noise – *ah!* – as though I had spoken the letter aloud. I would come to know that would always hurt a little, to write.

My grandfather believed that even if women could know scripture, they could never learn to read the verses, only to hear them and thereby consecrate them to memory. He said this was because of an innate female capacity for the same. To absorb.

But when Padmamma began to bring me scraps of writing to read to her – unbound palm leaves from almanacs, miscellanea from parchments found in temples, something that had fallen into her wares in the marketplace, carried amongst a trader's wares from another village – I watched her curiosity and diffidence and understood. One day, as an experiment, I lied to her. I replaced all the nouns in a line. Papaya became bitter gourd, the sun became the moon. She continued to listen as though nothing was out of place, processing the words I spoke without question, watching my finger as it underlined the lines. She never dared to pick up a bound or complete text, although we had many in our home. These scraps were all she felt were permissible for her to look at, and through me she had access to them.

Once I saw what it means for a woman to be writless, I began to devour words with the knowledge that this was the only miracle of my life – to have them. To know them, and myself through them. To recognize them on sight. First, Vishnuchittan taught me how to read and then allowed me to take his materials – his holy texts and his own poetry and others', collected from temples and bartered for from traders – even without his supervision. As for Amma, she neither dictated things to be written down nor did she take particular notice of the presence of calligraphy anywhere. In this way, she maintained concord with the ways of my grandparents. Of her own parents, she rarely spoke.

But on some nights, my mother and father would linger a little while on the thinnai, our clean-swept front porch with room enough for a pilgrim to sleep on, after lighting a brazier of neem leaves to ward away insects, waiting for my grandparents and me to fall asleep. And I would be able to hear his lilting voice read to her. Softly. I could see his small lantern burning if I turned my head just so from my mat. I could never hear or see my mother's reactions, but years later when the verses of the *Kuruntokai* broke in me a dam I did not even know I contained, I could imagine them. How it must have been for her to be offered words strung together like garlands, their sentiments so vital even after a thousand years that bees would still spin intoxicated if they heard them. Later, I would come to envy her. For I was certain she had never known it, what it was like to weep until the place between her breasts filled up with tears, became a pond where a black-legged white heron fed, how it felt to have her whole body turn into a landscape where life thrives, tenacious, but in the absence of touch.

2

Before Vishnuchittan became my father, he was already a mother.

Each morning before sunrise, Vishnuchittan bathed quietly at the well and entered the groves, smelling of the bark he had scrubbed his body with. He plucked leaves of tulasi for the day's garland and selected from the flowering shrubs the colours that would interweave their green. Jasmine was his favourite, for its scent as well as for the way the white petals looked nestled in the leaves. He would carry what he gathered back to the house, where he would sit on the thinnai and begin his work, his stomach empty but for water. He used only the tips of his fingers to knot each stem and bud into a banana fibre twine, working quickly, the garland emerging from his hands. His nose and mouth would be covered with a piece of cloth so that he would not inhale the fragrance of the verdure and partake of its pleasure before the lord took his. And then, he would walk down past his father's fields to the Vatapatrasayi temple and offer this garland to Maha Vishnu in his form as the lord who sleeps on a banyan leaf.

Vishnuchittan was a boy when he began this morning ritual, and that was also when he began fighting his father, the Acharya, on what God wanted of him.

In those days, the grove was still a part of our family's agrarian land. My grandparents, before they became my grandparents, grew produce – yams, bananas, varieties of spinach and gourds, depending on the year and its season. Tulasi grew only in one section, along with flowering plants. These were for worship alone.

My father, the son of a priestly teacher, wanted only to knot garlands for his god and to sing to him. When he closed his eyes, verses came to him whole, and in them he loved his lord like a mother does her child. He sang for his Krishna – his Vatapatrasayi, his Narayana, his Vishnu by one name or many – in the voice of Devaki, the woman who gave her boy up before she could nurse him so that he could live, far from the treachery of her household.

Visnuchittan told his own mother that he had no need for progeny, and he told his father that he had no need for dogma.

Then one day, a woman with hair like thunderclouds and skin as dark as a young mango leaf visited Puduvai with her own father, and chose not to return with him to the place she came from. She brought with her a sweet dialect, a blue-green diagram tattooed on her forearm, and a tendency to speak too much or not at all. The

Acharya had begun to grow old by then, and could do nothing but sulk. His wife, my grandmother Padmamma, named for the lotus, welcomed the younger woman into her home as she had accepted all else that had changed in the decades since her own wedding, with the rue of knowing that she had no say. Crops that nourished had been uprooted for holy plants. A son she had raised to stand apart from the crowd wandered the town like a mendicant, flowers wilting behind his ear like a woman, one shoulder branded with the icon of the discus, the other with the icon of the conch. She had long given up hope that he would bring home a wife. Padmamma told me once – sometime after Mukunda Acharya had died in his sleep, a little under a decade after I was found in the tulasi grove – how her new daughter-in-law's eyes had lit up upon seeing the baby calves, and how that was when something in Padmamma's tired heart had softened.

Sixteen Aadi months have passed since I was found, and my father still makes his garland for Vatapatrasayi Perumal, every day. The grove is large, and some days when I have spent too much of the night there, I hide in its far reaches until my father returns to the house with his basket full. I lurk amidst the overgrown vines and hope he does not see me. But I cannot wait too long, for I cannot risk Padmamma or Amma waking to see that I am not between them on the mats. I fix myself quickly and quietly, and make my way to the large window I always leave imperceptibly ajar, its hinges always kept oiled, and climb in through the side of the house. In my peripheral view is my father, who sits on the thinnai at the front of the house and knots his garland as the sky begins to lighten slowly. In this small house in this small town, however small my being, I cannot possibly go unnoticed. We simply never speak of it. This man, who was a mother before he became my father, becomes both and neither in his silence. I re-enter the house and prepare for my own bath just as my mother and grandmother begin to wake. And when my father brings the garland to me for its first rite, there is nothing in his eyes that implies doubt of any kind, nothing on his tongue but a litany of his faith. I step out to milk one of our cows and wait for the cowherds to arrive, the first heat of the day on my back. My father leaves for the temple, a tray held before him bearing his offering to the lord.

Once, our little town and its surroundings were led by a queen whose name means jasmine, the flower that blooms more propitiously here than anywhere else. This is all we know of her: that she was Rani Malli, and that her two sons were Villi and Kandan, one named for the hunt – that activity that at once is war and play, succour and sport – and one named for the warrior god who is the patron of the Tamil people. One day, on a hunt, the princes became separated somewhere in the thickness of the forest. Villi did not know that his brother was killed by a tiger until, at the end of a day of searching for him, he fell into a slumber in which Kandan's fate was divinely revealed in a dream. Along with this revelation was an instruction: to build a city.

Growing up, I loved hearing stories, any stories, because I could understand neither my mother's silence about where and who she came from nor my grandfather's insistence that only what he said could be true. In some tellings of this story of the origin of Puduvai, Kandan is returned to life; in other tellings, beneath the rock on which Villi dreams is an idol of Vishnu-Krishna reclining on a banyan leaf. But there are not any tellings that I know of in which Rani Malli appears again. Even still, I want for this story to be true only so I can know for certain that even amongst the strongholds of the kingdoms of Tamilagam, there were women who ruled.

Villi built Puduvai, close enough to the capital of Madurai to still be jasmine country, but far enough so that even now, the ways of the city don't interfere in our simple rural ways. It was in Madurai that Vishnuchittan spoke in the royal court so eloquently that his rivals conceded that his worship was greater than their own paths. This is a story that I love, and a story that he loves repeating. Somewhere in the years between becoming a holder of the scriptures and becoming my father, the lord appeared to Vishnuchittan in a dream and told him to participate in a religious debate that would be judged by Raja Srimara Srivallabha, who sits to this day on the throne of the Pandya kingdom.

This maker of garlands, who had devoted his life to nothing more than twine and constant meditation, paid for passage in a trader's bullock cart and arrived at the palace without expectation. He would tell me much later that he could never be sure why the kings revelled in these philosophical disputes, because nothing remains in the realm of thought alone. A defeated man brings his humiliation back into his own place of worship, and when he hears the name of another's god, is reminded of this defeat. He sweats his defeat as he walks through his town. The soil becomes sowed with the way his defeat makes him feel. The wind folds the scent of it into itself. And one day, another man raises his sickle because of a defeat he did not even know existed. And spilled blood too seeps into the soil, becomes a part of what its natives eat, bathe in, believe.

My father was not humiliated, and perhaps that it is why everything he tends flourishes. Or perhaps it was because he was already like that, without ambition, that he was not defeated in the first place.

In Madurai that day, half a dozen men each spoke before the king on the greatness of their chosen deity, and how their path was the one that could ease all human suffering. When it came to my father's turn, he nervously began to expound the teachings Mukunda Acharya had conveyed to him. The scriptures he was versed in were in Sanskrit, the language of the gods that only high-born men were permitted to know. The same scriptures which, if heard by a woman or man of a labouring caste, demanded the pouring of molten lead into the ears on which they had fallen. But when Vishnuchittan spoke them, they came from the tongue of a man who wore a crossbelt, the thread of the priestly caste, and because of this alone these words were praised and received with fear by his competitors. And then, just when he would have won anyway, my father quietened for a moment and sang. In soft, sweet Tamil. A verse from a poet named Satagopan of the city of Kurugur who had lived and died in the previous century, cocooned within a tamarind tree like a nesting bird. He was a devotee of Vishnu who had been born into the fourth strata of the pyramid of birth, whose family would not have owned the fields they tilled.

He sang: 'My lord of a thousand names gives and gives. The fame of his giving crosses all boundaries. I cannot praise anyone else, cannot say to some paltry thing in this world: "Your hand is as bounteous as the rain. Your shoulders are as strong as the mountain." I cannot tell such barefaced lies.'

The verse had emerged from his throat without his volition. Panic seized his breath. He had insulted the king.

But Raja Srimara Srivallabha did not notice it, or could not parse an insult within language so beautiful. Around him, the court erupted in applause, for there was no one who could not understand those words, who could have found them so foreign or so lofty as to merely agree to them in uncomprehending awe.

Vishnuchittan was given a title, Pattarpiran, the Leader of the Learned, and a silken bag of gold coins so heavy he wished he could place it on the ground. Then the king asked that he ride an elephant through the streets of Madurai, so every citizen could see the great man who had spoken so persuasively about the power and compassion of Maha Vishnu. Raja Srimara Srivallabha, unlike his father before him, gravitated towards this deity and not Siva, the god with a crescent tangled in his dreadlocks that most Pandya kings loved, or towards the mother goddess, in whose lap the people in the deepest forests and villages lay their hearts and their entreaties, and from whose bosom the city of Madurai sprouted. He was delighted that the debater who had spoken on behalf of his own favourite divinity had possessed such intelligence and eloquence.

Vishnuchittan had never mounted an elephant in his life. The great beast, trained for supplication in a manner that my father recognized was his own, bent her knees and lay her trunk at his feet. He lowered his head, and the elephant understood. She lifted her trunk and placed it lightly on his head. Then he accepted the mahout's help and threw one leg over a saddle decorated with bright embroidery, steadied himself, and drew his breath in as he rose to a height he had never experienced before.

Every street in the city radiated outwards from the temple at its centre, dedicated to the emerald goddess, Meenakshi of the fishlike eyes. The elephant swayed gently through these streets, and Vishnuchittan was fascinated by their bustle. He could see the ripple of the city's commotion from a minor distance, but it ceased as soon as he drew near, for the people of the city approached with jasmines to throw along his path, setting aside the trades, arguments, gossip or duties they had been preoccupied with just minutes before. Joy washed over him, along with the memory of his dream and awe at the honour that heeding it had brought him.

Then he heard the piercing cry of an eagle, so loud that he thought it was near his head. And when he looked up, he saw, closer than the clouds, his Maha Vishnu, right there, flanked by two consorts, riding his bird mount just as Vishnuchittan himself rode the king's elephant.

Vishnuchittan swooned. The reins nearly slipped from his grip, but he came to his senses when the tiny bells tied to them began ringing. He began to sing, tears pouring down his face. 'For many years, for thousands of years, for hundreds of millions of years, may the red feet of the lord of sapphire hue be protected… May the praising of Narayana last a very long time.'

The vision dissolved only as he came to the last verse. Vishnuchittan was filled with all the world's grief and all the world's rapture as he climbed gently from the elephant's back to bow to the king, who bowed in return to him. He wept through the night in a bullock-drawn cart to Puduvai. He remained inconsolable until the following morning, when once more he walked into what were then still his father's fields and plucked with gentle fingers tulasi leaves and orange jasmine, wove them into a garland, and carried this to the statue in the womb of the temple. His tears dried only when he saw the flame offering being lifted to illuminate and circle the face of his smiling god, a wreath made by his own hands hanging over his heart.

Soon after, Mukunda Acharya's fields ceased to be his, and his authority in his household began to yield. His son had moved the Pandyan king himself to prostrate before him. His son had sat on the monarch's own saddle and been paraded through the greatest city in the world.

Most importantly, his son had a bag of gold coins, and he handed it over to his father in exchange for unchallenged dominion over every fertile acre. Mukunda Acharya took the gold as security, since he knew not what his mad son would do next. He had no use for gold, said Vishnuchittan, for how could it compare to a grove, living and lush?

3

Tiruthulai, sacred basil, comes in seven forms that I know of. As Rama tulasi, its leaves are light green and asymmetrical. As Krishna tulasi, it is dark, purple-hued, with potent medicinal qualities. As Vana tulasi, named for the forests, it can grow to the height of a small tree, its velvety fronds broad and sun-seeking. As Kapoor tulasi, purple-red flower clusters sprout from between green leaves. Less sacred basil grows in the distant continent of the cross-bearers, and rumour is that the taste of those leaves is sweet. It grows also, lemon-scented, beyond the sea in the lands to the south east, where its leaves, and all its sisters', are cooked to flavour curries for meat and fish.

The seventh form is as consort, goddess in the guise of a plant, incarnated to remind the householder of the holiness of the very dirt that keeps him rooted. She exists like an aura in all the visible other forms, and she is the one we hold in our minds as we circle her in worship, or drink her as a tonic for ailments of the chest and throat. We ask for her forgiveness each time we pluck a leaf.

They also say that she tastes bitter because bitterness is what conceived her. They say her leaves are the tears that Vishnu shed after the cosmic ocean was churned, when the world was created through the equal participation of greed and good. They say she was a woman married to a demon, and after he was killed, she climbed into her husband's pyre. They say that out of her ash came root and petiole, lush and fragrant. I say that whatever else she may be, she is my sister too, for I was brought into this world beside her, in the luxuriant shelter of her arms, and that in me too is bitterness and in me too is beauty, and in me too, is the capacity to heal, and to bless and to blessed be.

4

Sometimes I sit on our thinnai as dusk descends and wonder if, anywhere in the world, there is another like me. There is certainly no one like me in Puduvai, but then Puduvai is small, a village in the foothills of a great mountain range, where in certain slants of light the shadow of Madurai falls.

If I could walk for a little over an hour to the west, I will enter Shenbaga Thoppu, the vast coppice of magnolia trees, which then opens onto a forest and the first crowns of the mountains that divide us from the Chera country. There are waterfalls in that wilderness, and strange trees, and places where both butterflies and tigers roam elegantly and without dispute. Honey-hives sag heavily like drupes of palmyra beneath the overhangs of cliffs. Squirrels take brief and death-defying flights, while birds dip their long beaks into cool, running water and idle. Monkeys fight over fruits as though the branches they swing from are not abundant with them. I could pick up a red mango, freshly fallen, dust it off and eat it as I walked. I could enter streams and have tiny black fish scatter away from me in fear. I could caress a deer, and follow its herd without care for the route back. I could take a lover behind the curtain of a waterfall, so its plunge drowns our cries of love. I could read in the light of the late afternoon, as the heat dries my clothes and my hair. I could pluck a flower that doesn't grow in my father's garden, and wear it home like a triumph, or fold its seeds into a leaf to gift to him. If I *could* walk for a little over an hour to the west… If I could go neither escorted nor in secret.

I have done this – gone to Shenbaga Thoppu, alone – only in times when my father has travelled, when the task of weaving and then wearing the garland of the lord has been mine, and the day has stretched ahead with little reproach.

I long for these places, for the right to leave for them at will, for a household that belongs to me alone and will confront me with no questions upon my departure or my return. My father's orchard is not enough for me, not enough for the bird in my throat to be free.

Beyond those mountains is the abundantly fertile Chera kingdom, from which the greater world buys its spices. Sometimes when I smell or touch certain ingredients, I wonder at how they have travelled farther than I may ever will.

There is nothing in Puduvai that cannot be found elsewhere in Tamilagam. But at least we know of that greater world, and on some unusual occasions that world knows of us too. There are stories I have gathered, eavesdropping in the marketplace, of things I have never seen but want so much to believe are true. Once, a bearded man passed through on a horse, carrying with him a coded message he was forbidden to read, tempting a punishment of death if he did. Once, a scholar who spoke Tamil with difficulty visited, and spoke it only to priests and men employed by the empire that had approved his passage. Once, a woman with red hair and skin that was like milk flecked with blood passed by late in the night; she had taken shelter on a thinnai and custom forbade that she be disturbed, but by morning she was gone, leaving a smokelike rumour for years afterwards.

To the north and the south are looms and architecture, literature and maritime expeditions, and the aegis royal and divine that allows each to prosper. Every empire has something that reflects its glory, and the small towns bask in it like the moon basks in solar light. So in Puduvai we say: we are close to the grand city of Madurai, where the Vaigai swells, bringing from the hills the essences of cardamom, teakwood and the kokilam creeper in its waters; the city where the last of the three sangams of the ancient poets of Tamilagam was convened.

I have never been to Madurai; I too bask only in reflected glory, my father's. Sometimes when I close the books containing those ancient poems, a sadness filled with questions rises in me.

Here, in this tiny town in which the flag of the Pandyan fish also flies, we have nothing that might make someone far away dream of us, as I dream of them and the fabric of their lives, except for our Vatapatrasayi temple. It is a story that draws the pilgrims here – never women without men, and each man with a long line drawn between his eyebrows, the lord marked on his skin with mica, turmeric mixed with lime juice or sandalwood. Vishnu in his form as Varaha, the boar, dove into the primordial ocean, where Bhu, the goddess who is this planet and the element of earth, had been held hostage. Having killed the golden-eyed demon who tormented her, Vishnu-Varaha placed his tusks beneath her waterlogged body and raised her out of those depths. And then, he rested: beneath a banyan tree, on the bed of a banyan leaf, here in the place where this temple now stands.

And that is why they come here, the men and their families who sleep on the thinnais of strange houses and drop coins into the coffer outside the temple. These coins allow the temple to feed and to teach, and for those in the priestly quarters to, in turn, keep our houses and our own open porches. Vatapatrasayi is the lord in a form that is said to be unusual: the baby Krishna, asleep on a fig leaf, sucking on the sweetness of his own big toe. Devaki's child, who was not suckled by his mother, who my father adopted as his own just as he did me.

Only, the deity inside the temple is neither boar-god nor beautiful child, but the lord grown and magnificent, reclining on his serpent, a banyan tree at his head. He occupies the upper storey of this temple, a flight of steps leading us to his form – supine, at rest after battle, just as the lord at Tiruvarangam – a place I long to see – is said to be. Sometimes when I stand in front of him, my mind wanders to the place where what I am told loses alignment to what I see before me. This must mean that within stone is a secret, of what happened to the original idol – or the original story.

But below, on the level of the earth, is something fiercer, darker, more primal. Here, Vishnu presides as the lion with the lower body of a man. Narasimha. The folds of the fabric he wears still bearing what spilled when he tore a demon on his knee and took its intestines for a garland. His ferocity tempered by the loveliness who sits on his lap, consort and plenipotentiary. Lakshmi. I who was born when the stars cast his shape across the sky long to live as she does, so close to his fierce breath, his rumbling chest.

With my family, I stand before Vatapatrasayi Perumal and chant like the good child of a priestly family, as respectful as the two consorts who stand at his feet. I adore his long body and the seduction of his posture, openly. But before Lakshmi-Narasimha, I am always speechless. It is him I go and see when fears churn in me, and when unnameable desires and doubts assail me. And when I have taken my fill of his power, when he has cleansed me of confusion, it is his beloved who I yearn to be, enthroned on the blood-strewn benediction of his lap.

My father's first small garden, the far corner of the grove in which I was found amongst tendrils of tulasi, adjoins this temple. In the dark of the night, when the doors of each shrine have been closed and no one walks the stone floors, I can still hear from within it the soft tinkle of bells, and the smell of freshly-lit frankincense wafts towards me on the northern wind, intertwining with the scents of wet leaves and magnolias closer to me. My consort is in the near distance, and my fingertips coax flower, song and fire from deep within me.

I cannot go there only at night, during malefic daytime hours and when eclipses mar the sky. But even in the most auspicious of times, not everyone is allowed to enter this temple. Even in the largest city of Tamilagam, the seed of the smallest village is contained, and here in this miniscule town the laws are as inescapable as anywhere else. The world is divided into layers of worthiness. They say you cannot challenge what you were born into. I cannot even challenge what I was not born into, even if it claimed me with a legend as beautiful as a garland of tulasi, pinned through with string, a perfect offering. But who knows whose blood reigns in my veins, animates the pulses of my wrists, at my throat, within my storm-drenched and blazing heart?

There are other temples in Puduvai. Always, to the mother goddess whose body takes the forms of snake hills, margosa leaves and lime fruit. To the princely one who holds his vel, the spear with a blade ovate like an eye or a leaf. To his father, who is the consort of the mother goddess, whose deepest beloveds wear their hair in long matted ropes just like him, their skin covered with ash. And also, to the parrot-rider Kamadeva, who carries a bow strung with flowers, who was incinerated then resurrected bodiless, who is the season of spring. He is the god of lust and romantic love, the god of coupling, the god of the pleasures of the body. I go to his temple in secret on afternoons when the sanctum is closed but the town is asleep. And I lift the veil that covers him and disturb him, and I look at him eye to eye, and I ask for his permission, and I demand his grace.

5

I do not envy anyone like I envy the young women who tend the cows, who wear their garments hiked up to the knee to allow them to squat to milk their beloved beasts; who sometimes bare their torsos under the sun when they bathe in groups by the lotus lake, when they labour in summer far from the gazes of those who have the opulence of working under roofs and awnings, and even when all they want is to have their skin be kissed by the wind. I have seen them. I have followed them to their homes as a child, taking advantage of my mother's busyness and tolerance. I have watched them knot their garments above their breasts as they entered the water then allowed the cloth to loosen, as though they didn't notice. Maybe they didn't. They laugh like no one has ever told them not to. Their teeth shine frequently in their bright faces. And they pluck flowers for themselves and for each other, without waiting for a man to bring some to them, and adorn their wrists and coiffures with verdure as if they have never needed to be told they are beautiful.

They are beautiful.

When my grandfather – Mukund Acharya, the teacher of priests – was still alive, the cowherds were not permitted to even stand by our front door, let alone enter our house. Even if something was needed, they had to wait outside the kitchen door at the back and call to Padmamma, who then handled the matter or relayed it to the men of the house. This practice began to lose its grip after Vishnuchittan's victory at the court of Raja Srimara Srivallabha, but it wasn't until after the Acharya's demise that it truly ended.

There were other practices that went unchallenged for a long time. As a child, I observed how Amma was never permitted to serve the Acharya his food or drink, even if it may have been her who prepared it. So Padmamma would have to hobble with her bad leg from the kitchen to her husband's quarters, and back to fetch him more water, and then to collect his used plantain leaf, and finally to bring him buttermilk. After which he slept and she rested by his side, waiting for his next command. My grandfather loved me, but because he never forgot who he was, he never allowed me to be anything but who he wanted me to be. What would that love have been if not for that mitigation? Now, when I massage Padmamma's tired back with herbed oil and she scowls at how I wander all over town whenever I can, I don't find it in me to become angry. Some of the things she believes are like the knotted places in her body, tightened from both disuse and abuse. They are not who she is, either.

Amma has never been as strict as my grandparents or even Vishnuchittan – whose lenience does not extend beyond the home and the temple – about what I do with my time. Sometimes, after we have sold the seasonal produce yielded by the tamarind and banana trees and the few remaining crops in the fields, she will ask me to buy our own rations while she visits a friend or runs another errand, fetching a poultice for aching limbs or buying goods which have to be procured from beyond the marketplace. When I go to a temple with her, she does not always ask me to account for what I do while she idles in conversation in its compound. And even through the day, as long as my chores are completed, she does not check on how I spend my hours. I think it is a kind of surveillance she herself detested, for once Padmamma began to be less able to use her legs, I saw how some tension melted in Amma. She too became freer. 'Some women have wider cages than others,' she said to me once, after a bitter morning. Still, I feel the boundaries of mine all the time.

One day, a travelling couple brought their wares to Puduvai. They had not sold their stock entirely in Madurai, and were loathe to burden their bullock cart with the remainder for long. They came from a coastal place, and had also wanted to see the mountains. And so they hoped to not have to carry their goods into the ghats. That afternoon, they spread ornaments and beads on a large cloth in our market. Coral pendants and earrings, tree bark chiselled into shapes that wound around the wrists and fingers, shells strung with colourful threads, mirrors around which pebbles were assembled, probably using an animal adhesive my grandfather would have forbidden me to touch. The only thing they did not have were pearls. I knew this even before I drew close, for the woman was talking to a customer.

'To buy pearls one must be wealthy. To sell pearls one must be a wealthy trader,' she smiled. 'You must be wealthy, sir, but I am not. What I can offer you are only baubles, but they are still made with love.'

The customer moved along. My eye and heart had already become fixed on something so beautiful it made my throat dry with longing. Conch bangles. They glowed on the fabric they lay on, a pair of smooth white spheres against bright redness.

I knelt without grace and picked them up before anyone else might sight them. 'What do these cost?'

'Those,' said the woman, 'are not for sale.'

'Then why are they here?'

The man said something to her in another language, something I could only catch scraps of.

'My mistake,' he reached over. 'I didn't mean to keep them out there.'

'I would really like to buy these from you,' I insisted, still holding the bangles.

'What will you do with them?'

'Why, wear them of course.'

'And will you sing the glory of Keshava as you do?' He seemed to be laughing.

This confused me. The woman shushed the man and looked at me. 'The one who made these bangles told us they were meant to be a gift. We cannot sell them. Please understand.'

I had tears in my eyes. 'A gift for whom?'

Just then my mother appeared by my side. 'Kodhai! Where have you been?'

'For the one who sings the glory of Keshava,' said the man.

'That would be me. That *is* me,' I said.

And then my strange mother said a few words to the couple in their own language, and the man's eyes brightened. 'Is it true?' he asked me in Tamil.

'What is?'

'That the lord of this town wears a garland only after you have worn it yourself?'

'Yes.' I straightened my back. 'It is true.'

'And do you sing?' smiled the woman.

'I... do.' I said cautiously. Well. I decided that I could. No – I decided that I would.

The couple grinned at my mother. The woman asked her something. My mother didn't reply, shaking her head ambiguously.

'All right, little girl,' said the man. 'You keep them then.'

'I will buy these earrings too.' My mother reached for a pair made of coral beads stacked on a slim line of metal curved into a teardrop shape.

'Oh, you don't have to, sister,' said the woman. This I understood.

My mother insisted. She squatted and picked other baubles: a small mirror, a comb made of shell, a second pair of earrings made of wood. She unknotted the end of her sari and took out a coin. Heat rose in my face. I had been rash, of course, to have thought I could barter these bangles for our own stock, with unripe bananas or a bouquet of foxtail millet or a rope of hill garlic, pungent and earth-stained.

The woman from the coast wrapped my mother's purchases in a plantain leaf and pushed a twig through the ends to make a bundle. Meanwhile, I slipped a hand into each bangle. The left one, then the right one. They were heavy and cool to the touch. They were too big for me then, but I would thicken them with twine. I didn't think I would ever take them off.

Once, not so many years ago, I followed the cowherds to their part of town as they went home for their afternoon meals. I had already eaten, and my family were at rest. This was the hour at which I was allowed to wander the fields or the neighbouring compounds, my mother perfectly aware that the heat would draw me back quickly.

I think they knew that I was there, shadowing them at a short distance, but no one chastised me. They lived not so many streets and fields away, but it's funny how precisely hierarchy can fold a town or village down to its most petty proportions.

I have never really had friends of my own age. The love of my parents and grandparents took up most of my heart – then as now – and where it did not, my own love for the lord filled the silent spaces like water fills fractured earth. There were neighbours, certainly. Some of them were children too, even the ones who were already married and waiting to be old enough to move to their mothers-in-law's homes. And it is not as though I did not climb mango trees with them or play mancala games with them, using the tamarind seeds and shallow holes we scooped into the soil. It is not as though I was always alone. Just often. And it is not as though no one asked me why I was not already betrothed, or revealed in their eyes that they thought they knew why.

I adored most of the cowherds separately and I adored them even more collectively. They were the only young women I saw every day, for the women and girls of my own quarter were usually cloistered. The men and women of their clan did the same work, and there was something about the cowherds I knew that always seemed to belong to some other era, a time when one married for love and not by decree of a horoscope. I would come to articulate this only later, when my father allowed me to read the ancient anthologies, in which women's voices rang clear, in tones dulcet and demanding, yearning without shame. I was angry then that I had been gifted neither: a creed of fewer codes, or the permissiveness of another century.

The cowherds' quarter is by a lake, its shore clustered with trees. That afternoon, I sat under one and yellow blossoms floated down to me in the wind. I fell asleep this way, and when I woke I was in my own home, on a mat on the floor. It was as though I had dreamt it all: walking that distance, the narrowing paths, the summer heat, the way the sunlight rippled on the lake water and long grasses dipped their heavy heads gently along its border. But I know that could not have been true. Someone had carried me home that afternoon, and I had made all those journeys, in secret and in slumber. There is no sea in Puduvai. I have never stepped into the ocean. But somewhere on the cusp between experience and illusion is a shining lake. And there are conch bangles on my wrists. I wear my saris hiked to the knee. I tend cows. I laugh with all my teeth. I fall into love, and out of love, I blossom. This is where I spent my whole childhood escaping to in my imagination. It is the one gift I am sure that Mayavan, he of the worldly illusion, did not deprive me of.

6

The first time that my body released the blood of the moon, I had been wearing white garments. And when I unclothed myself as I prepared to bathe, I admired what I saw for a few moments before I realized what it was. To me, the vivid stain on the white cloth looked like the crimson inner heart of a white hibiscus. I longed suddenly to place my finger within its folds, the place from which its stamen would shoot out, so flamboyant that it would loll under the weight of its own adornments.

Amma had told me this would come, a long time ago, when one of the young cowherds had come running from the shed in tears to find her. The girl had stood hovering outside the threshold, panic-struck, pointing wordlessly to the blood that was running down her leg. I must have been eight years old or so then. Half a lifetime ago.

When mine came, a little over a year ago, I took that first blood stained cloth to Amma, who embraced me with a relief I hadn't expected. She said then that she had been worrying about why it had taken so long. We called Padmamma, who wept as she thought she should, but could not say why when I asked her.

Vishnuchittan was delighted. Our closest neighbour's younger daughter, who was not even as old as I was, had moved into her in-laws' home recently, having already been married since childhood. It occurred to me that her moon blood must have come in the months before. They had held no ceremony to announce or acknowledge it, but my parents wanted to do so for me.

'It's almost like a wedding,' Amma said joyfully. 'You'll be dressed almost like a bride.'

'And there should be a wedding not long after,' reminded Vishnuchittan.

Padmamma was more circumspect. 'Is it really necessary for all the town to know that she has come of age? Is it not a little…' She looked at me, lips pursed. 'You decide.'

I decided I wanted it: the ceremony of flowers that marked my entry into womanhood, that told the world I was a woman before any man could make me one.

When the day came, my mother and grandmother dressed me in yellow brocade. I was bathed in turmeric, so my skin was stained golden for days. Lit camphor placed on a coconut was circled in front of me as handheld bells rang clear, as though I was a goddess and not just a girl. Our small house was full of women: women who barricaded doorways unwittingly with their chatter and their hips, women with their mouths and palms full of sweets, women with their thick jasmine-braided hair, women with their voices tinkling like many pendants on a single loop of silver. I had become one of them too, and all of them knew it.

Some came with their mothers-in-law if they weren't allowed to otherwise. Some came with their babies in their bellies or held like mud pots on the cambers of their waists. A few came with their young daughters, a mixture of worry and pride in their eyes. But it was only the women who mattered, no matter who their companions were. This many women, at once, celebrating womanliness.

When I had been bathed in turmeric water and dressed in fresh clothes, my eyes lined again with collyrium, the guests gathered around me. Huge baskets overflowing with blossoms and vines encircled me and held me at the centre of a consecrated diagram on the earth. Our house was too small to hold so many people, and the grove too sacred to withstand such trampling, and so it was on the grounds in front of our home that this ceremony was held. Bullock-carts laden with produce passed by leisurely every once in a while. I sweated in my silks under the overcast sky. It was the season of the north-eastern monsoon, but thundershower had not yet flooded our fields fecund, washed the waiting from our thoughts, shattered the rice kolams at our thresholds and mingled grain back into earth.

A hush fell on the crowd as my mother began humming. A sweet, low timbre. She held hairpins between her lips and so could not sing, but that was for my father to do anyway. Vishnuchittan sang one of his own compositions, a few earnest guests crooning along, as Amma patiently ornamented my braid with flowers and plants, crowning me with verdure.

My father became a mother in his songs. Krishna's mother, Devaki, who had held him in her body and then pushed him out of it, only to have him taken away from her. Devaki who never watches him grow. Never loses her temper at him. Never feels disappointed by him. Never loves him with balls of food mashed in her hands or kisses his hair till he sleeps after night terrors. She prays that he will never forget what it was like to live beside her heartbeat, to know her as no one else can from the inside. Vishnuchittan wrote the lullabies Devaki could never sing to him, her baby, and he sang them to me.

My father stood before me with tears in his eyes and sang the song of a mother begging her mischievous child to hold still so she could adorn him with the flowers she had so lovingly plucked for him as he had taken the cows to graze, teased milkmaids, stolen and greedily gobbled butter, reclined in the temple of Tiruvarangam, reclined in the heavenly abode of Vaikuntham, or reclined right here in this insignificant town, under the microcosmos of a banyan tree.

My mother tucked each botanic enticement that the lord's mother had tried to coax her child with into my hair, which she bundled and pinned to one side of my head. Magnolias – of course. Jasmine – but always. Bell-shaped pink flowers of the padri tree with green springs of the davanam creeper. The davanam again, this time accompanying the marjoram herb, with its tiny florets. Freshwater lotuses. The blossoms of the drupe-bearing beautyleaf tree. Kurukathi lianas. A second kind of jasmine, the thin-petalled iruvatchi. The lushly fragrant ylang-ylang flower, with its petals elongated and drooped like banana peels.

Honeybees and jewel-winged butterflies fluttered and hummed around my head, slipping their tongues into the centres of flowers with petals that still shimmered with dew-water. They caused me no injury, and I did not wave them away.

As he sang, the gathered women tossed petals over me, and in my imagination the flowers grew over me like an anthill, and I felt that I could meditate for a thousand years within their fragrance, until one day, a song set free from my throat would dispel that stillness. I would emerge in a farther century carrying all the history and libel and lore of this one. My body always sixteen years old, lush and life-bearing.

And even as they sang and swayed around me, I withdrew in my mind's eye to the sacred grove. In darkness, I would wait silently in the grass for the sound of his anklets, for he would come to me without taking them off, without deceit, without fear. I dreamt with my eyes open. And under all my layers of silk and foliage, beneath the cooling anointments of sandalwood and turmeric, in the place from which the blood of the moon had blossomed from my body, everything turned to nectar. I closed my eyes and summoned his image: chest like a mountain, navel sprouting a lotus, lips that I envied the conch in his hand for having kissed. Come to me. To me. Come.

7

After the ceremony celebrating my menarche, my family had begun to speak of the wedding to come. As the daughter of Pattarpiran, the Leader of the Learned, who received the patronage of Raja Srimara Srivallabha, I would be able to choose from a wide selection of suitors. Did I want to live in the capital, where I would never be bored? Did I want to live closer to our hometown, or even in it? (But was there a boy or young man of suitable age in this little place, one who could equal Vishnuchittan's Kodhai?) Did I want a man who was tall, or one with whom I could stand eye-to-eye? Did I want a man with dark skin like my mother's, or one whose skin was creamy like my father's? Or someone the shade of deerskin, like me, with whom I could have children sweet as sapotas?

Did I want a man who was a priest, and if not, was I prepared for what the priests would say?

Did I want to have a small house, or a big one, and how often would I come to visit my grandmother and my parents? Did I want to have sons or daughters, or both – and how many? Did I want to wear red at my wedding or green? Jasmines in my hair or roses? What month would I marry in, and what fruit would be in season for the feast? What would happen if my man didn't pray? What would happen if he prayed – but decided he wanted to become a Jain or a Buddhist or a Kaumara?

Amidst all these thrilling speculations, the one question that was never asked was whether or not I wanted a marriage. The truth is, I wanted a wedding. I had wanted to be a bride since I was a child. But I did not want what marriage meant: a belly that spilled loosely, a tightness between the brows when talking to younger women, a pair of lowered eyes around the in-laws. These are some of the things I saw in the bodies and faces of women of my father's caste, who were not permitted to leave their households without permission or to earn a living. If I did not find a man for myself, it had been made clear – even amidst the camaraderie of so many questions – an arrangement would be made with another family affiliated with the temple. And if none of the men in Puduvai were suitable, branches of those families were certain to extend further, to towns and villages beyond.

I had no assurance that such a man would listen to me recite my poems by the light of clay lanterns, as my mother had done with my father in the neem-scented nights of my childhood. That he would give me what the grove gave me. That he wouldn't envy my devotion, or turn bitter about my incapacity to offer the same to him. That I would not wilt under the canopy of his name. I could never be such a wife. But I wanted to be a bride: garlanded, gorgeous, radiant with the knowledge that come nightfall she will be entered, illumed, broken whole.

One evening, I sat on the step of the kitchen door – the women's porch – and watched as three cowherds walked their wards back through the long dirt path, their shadows lengthening along it. I could recognize them from afar from their shapes and gaits: Animalar, tall and slender, Kayalvizhi, whose left arm did not sway as she walked, and Matatilli of the hips like a wooden spinning top. I hoped they would have the time to talk to me today, that their own homes did not beckon them away too quickly.

In the gathering darkness, I could not see their faces until they were almost at the cowshed. 'Kodhai!' called Matatilli. 'You're going to be eaten by fever-carrying mosquitoes. Go inside, kannamma.'

'No, I've been waiting for you,' I called back, a little softly in case my grandmother somewhere in the rooms behind me stirred, curious.

In a few minutes they were tying the cows back into their places, enjoying the excitement of the calves. Matatilli picked a calf up and hoisted it on her shoulders. She reached one cupped hand above her and gently found the top of its head, rubbing between its ears. She smiled at me. She was almost ten years older than me but had never married. On either side of her nose were the tiniest rivets of metal, which caught all manner of light.

Animalar was the youngest, not even fifteen, her elbows still bony. Kayalvizhi was a mother of two, and somewhere between my age and Matatilli's. I knew that the both of them would not be able to tarry for long. I kept my eyes on Matatilli. She held my gaze and smiled again.

'Animalar, your parents will be waiting for you,' she said.

'I'll walk with you,' Kayalvizhi said to the girl, and Animalar reluctantly finished stacking the mud pots. 'I must be leaving too. Matatilli Akka, what about you?'

'I won't be long,' Matatilli replied. 'You two go ahead.'

The other two began to walk away. We watched them, and the descending dusk. The sun was a deep marigold colour, sinking and sinking. A flock of kuyils fluttered overhead, identifiable by their coos.

Matatilli squatted and leaned over to feel the embroidery on the borders of my sari. Then she leaned back on her haunches and smiled broadly.

'Will you tell me or will you not?'

'How are you, Akka? What's happening?' I began.

'I asked you a question, girl.'

I rested my face in my forearms and sighed. 'Nothing, Akka. I just wanted to talk to you a bit.'

'Oho? Something about the festival you had at your house a few months ago?'

'No, not that...'

'Then what?'

A lump formed in my throat. I turned my face away as though to wave off a flying insect.

'What happens next?' I whispered.

Matatilli must have understood, because she glanced quickly behind me, as though to ensure we were out of earshot.

'Your parents are looking for a match aren't they?'

'That's not what I want.'

'What do you want?'

'How come you never had a match arranged?'

I waited for her to respond. When she finally did, she was looking at the tops of the silhouetted tamarind trees as she spoke. 'I was engaged once. My betrothed died of a snake bite three months before the wedding. I had already been with child, and my baby died in my womb from my shock. After that, no one asked, and I asked no one.'

This was startling. 'Oh god—' I ventured.

'You were still quite little then. I used to work for the Ramachandrans' cowshed then. But I couldn't stand the gossip around me after it all happened. So I came here. Your mother—,' she paused to smile. 'Your mother is not…'

She wasn't going to finish the sentence, nor did I need her to. I knew my mother was as peregrine to this domicile and its original ethos as I was.

'She is the loveliest woman,' Matatilli went on. 'And she has a daughter too lovely to be left to wilt on the vine. Do you have a lover?'

I blushed. 'No.'

'Do you want one?'

'Yes...'

'If you cannot find him in the marketplace, you will find him by the waterfalls. If you cannot find him by the waterfalls, you will find him in the temple. If you cannot find him in the temple, you will find him in the flour mill. If you cannot find him in the flour mill, you will find him in the weavers' quarters. If you cannot find him in Puduvai, you will find him in Madurai. And if not there, in the Chera country beyond the mountains. And if he is not to be found even there, then you will find him after the month of Margali, after you have completed the vow you made.'

'What vow?'

'So impatient!' She pinched my arm. 'I told you to search afar first.'

'You know my family doesn't let me go anywhere alone. I am not like you. I don't get to be so free.'

'Shush, you are too young to be bitter. And you don't know yet that freedom must be paid for, and with what.'

'With what?'

She smiled and stroked my hair. 'Try all the other things first. And if they don't work, I'll tell you then how you can begin to teach yourself how to live alone.'

'And the vow?'

'Ah, the vow.' She paused. 'The pavai nombu.'

'You have to tell me.'

'I'm going to tell you, child. Only I'm going to have to tell your grandmother that I told you, otherwise she will be furious.'

'Please, please, I'll keep it a secret.'

'You won't be able to, and anyway it's not such a secret. You see, the god Krishna who you pray to in your house had a wife, Nappinai, who was a cowherd lady like me. And among us cowherd ladies, those of us who long for love or for—,' she blushed now. She cleared her throat and continued. 'Those of us who long for love, we spend the coldest month of winter in worship of the mother goddess, asking her to make us like Nappinai, and bring to us men who will love us as Krishna loved her.'

I felt as though a peacock had suddenly swept in from a place of camouflage, tail unfolded, and rearranged the world with its resplendence.

'How do I make this vow, how do I keep it?'

'Go and ask your grandmother who Nappinai is. After that, let's talk again.' Matatilli stood up and brushed the earth from her beautiful hips. And then she tucked the loose end of her sari back into her waist and was gone.

8

This is the first rite of the garland that Vishnuchittan weaves every morning for Vishnu as Vatapatrasayi, the lord beneath the banyan tree: I wait by the prayer alcove inside the house, still shivering from the well water that hasn't dried in my hair and in the places where my skin folds; under my arms, under my breasts, between my legs. He gets up from the porch without allowing the garland to touch the floor or any part of his body but his fingertips. It is always heavy with tulasi, studded with colour, a different kind each day: bright crimson tigerclaw flowers, white and yellow carnations, blue blossoms of the virgin conch vine that unfurl like the most secret place on my body.

In the prayer alcove is a small brass statue of Krishna, and a square mirror, small enough to hold by the hand, large enough to look deeply into.

I take the garland from my father's fingertips, holding it in a way he does not – with the fullness of my palms and without fear. And I lower my head into its hoop so that the twine that's knotted at its top sits firmly on the nape of my neck. And then my father lifts the mirror so it faces me, and I gaze at myself – a bride in basil, eyes and brows freshly lined so they are as elongated as fish-tails, small gemstones flashing in either nostril, and a smile to rival the curve of the moon.

My reflection and I admire one another for a few moments, and then I lift the garland off myself and place it on the tray that Vishnuchittan holds ready, and this is what he carries with him to the temple, where the lord waits for his favourite ornament, his worn and well-loved garland.

I was still a child when my father had discovered my trespass. A single curling hair amidst strands of bright white jasmine.

In those days, Vishnuchittan would weave his garland and leave it hanging on a hook near the prayer alcove before stepping into the fields to supervise the morning's work. If this was not done before he left for the temple, the sun would be quite high by the time he returned home, and too much of the workers' time would have been lost. Truly, it took but a few minutes of his time to speak to the farmers and give his instructions or hear their concerns. Tulasi hadn't overrun his property then. For the sake of his child and his parents, for the sake of his wife and the roof under which he lay with her, and for the sake of his own belly, Vishnuchittan asked the lord to overlook this worldliness. Having finished his duty in the fields, he would wash his feet, hands and face by the well and retrieve the garland gently from its safekeeping, and then walk to the temple, bearing it on its own special tray.

On one such morning, I had woken early and been turned out of the kitchen by Padmamma for mewling too much when I knew that no food could be eaten before my father left for the temple. Sullen and hungry, I walked around the house looking for my father, who was not even there. I could hear my mother bathing by the well, and Mukunda Acharya was still asleep. Spurned so completely, I decided to drown my sorrows in the prayer alcove, to pray as loudly as possible that my real parents – the pearl trader from Korkai, the gypsy who told fortunes, the princess who loved a peasant, the famous wrestler who won himself a fiefdom, the temple dancer who had dedicated herself to God, the sculptor who escaped the king who wanted to blind him so he would never again make beauty like what had been bought from him – would come and find me.

But that magnificent garland hanging on the hook, tempting me with its lush leaves of tulasi, white tuberoses and buttery bell-like allamandas, made me forget all of my pain.

I knew my father made garlands. I did not know that he left them unattended.

I climbed the prayer alcove – oh how wrong this was, to place my feet upon it – and stole the garland from its knob. It was so much heavier than I imagined, and it smelled so wonderful. It was like the grove had been brought into our house. Just then, I caught sight of the mirror on the wall opposite me. I saw my face, my big eyes and the long line of vermillion between my brows. And I couldn't stop myself.

I climbed down carefully and went closer to the mirror. I could not see all of me in it, but it showed me myself down to my torso, and that was all I needed.

I lifted that precious garland over my head and wore it, and was overjoyed.

I knew I did not have much time before my father would return, and with great reluctance and equal haste, I removed the garland and returned it to its hook. Carefully, carefully, I climbed up the prayer alcove, returned it to its hook, and scampered back down.

And then I opened the doors of the alcove and whispered to him quickly, my dark cowherd god, my flute-player, 'Krishna, I have married you. I have made you mine.'

This went on for some days before my father discovered a strand of my hair in the garland and shouted in fury. First, he had believed it had to be one of his own, for who else but he ever handled the lord's garland? And then Amma, in her own irreverent way, reached out and plucked the hair which he held like a burning coal in his hand and said, 'It is not yours. This hair is crimped, look at it. It looks like Kodhai's.'

By the time my father returned from the fields, I was usually found trying to wake my grandfather up. Everyone had been surprised by my recent desire to wake up with my mother, but there was nothing to discourage in the habit. I would admire myself in the mirror, place the garland back on its hook, and then run into the other room and curl up beside my grandfather. This was where my parents found me that morning, pretending to have fallen back asleep.

'Kodhai!' My mother grabbed my arm and shook it. 'I know you are awake. What have you done?'

'Nothing, Amma!'

'Perumal's garland has a hair in it.'

'Nothing, Amma! I didn't do anything!'

'Leave the child alone, woman,' Mukunda Acharya grumbled in his sleep.

Amma pulled me up and marched me out of the room. My father, stone-silent, was waiting outside the door.

'Never, never, never again must this happen. Never, ever, ever again will I forgive you,' he said in the most terrifying voice I had ever heard. Low and cold, furious.

Once again, my father bathed. And once again, he went into his grove and made a garland with banana twine and basil leaves and the flower that came to his hand first. The prayer had already begun at the temple when he got there, breathless. The garland was but the final ornament. The lord was being bathed in cascades of milk when he arrived before his shrine, already praying that his errant child could be forgiven.

But when the garland was finally lifted over Vatapatrasayi's crown of granite, the camphor that had been lit at his feet went out.

The gathered worshippers gasped at the bad omen.

Vishnuchittan told me later that his heart had never pounded so loudly in his chest before.

He returned home a man bereaved, certain his family – his bricolage of chance lineages and faith above creed

– had fallen from grace. He would not speak to anyone through the day, having retreated into his grove and then finally falling asleep there. Much later, he told me he had eaten tulasi through the day, in repentance and to assuage his hunger, swallowing the leaves with water from the pond so as not to sully their holiness with his teeth.

But that night in the grove, resting close to the place where I had come into his life as a baby, Vishnuchittan had a dream.

Vishnu came to him in every guise he knew him in – as man-lion, as undine, as the king carrying a strung bow – and in the appearance he loved him best – as his Vatapatrasayi beneath a banyan tree, his sleeping baby Krishna. And the lord said to my father, in a voice that to him was perfectly familiar, 'Why did you not bring me the garland that Kodhai had worn? I do not want a garland that she has not touched.'

And the next day, Vishnuchittan summoned me to the prayer alcove and with his own hands placed the garland on my shoulders. And he picked me up so I could see its true length in the mirror. And he held me as proudly as the father of a bride, and it was a bride that I became each morning. His bride. That thunderdark deity's. I became the consort of that god who wants only to be draped by a garden-fresh garland that has first belonged to me – a garland that is sometimes decorated by my hair, and always scented by my body.

On the morning that I begin the pavai nombu, the vow to the goddess Katyayani that will bring me a man comparable to my god, I will meet my father in the alcove as I always have. And just as always, I will have been awake for hours already. Only, instead of furtively escaping to the grove, I bathed by the well at the back of the house in the depth of the night, with the circular moon bright above me, and rippling and reassembling on the water. It had not mattered if the sound of the water splashing woke my family. They all knew what I was going to do, what I had committed myself to for the thirty days and nights of the month of Margali, when Dhanusu, the constellation of the horse-legged man with an arrow aimed high, rises in the northern hemisphere.

I had waited for this month, through the monsoon that preceded it, when over and over Matatiili's promise had gathered and quivered in my heart like drops of water at the tip of a blade of grass. We are now in the deepest winter of the southern heartland.

By the time my father enters the grove to pluck leaves and blooms for the garland, I will have already completed the first day's ritual.

From the shock of well-water in the night, I make my way through the streets, far past the priestly quarters. My anklets chime with every step, but I have no need for subterfuge. Through much of my journey, I can see the moon. I turn corners and have it surprise me. I look for it and find it gone. By its light alone, I find my way into the thicket of trees by the lakeside in which the cowherds live.

I do not know which home is whose, which woman I know or don't know has drawn the remains of the rice flour mandala in front of its entrance on the morning before, now shattered by the night's winds and the day's visits.

And so I walk down to the water and wait, and before long I hear voices trying to be quiet, their timbres young and blithe, and then I sight Animalar's tall silhouette emerging down the snaking path. There are two others with her, and one of them wears a skirt shot through with tiny mirrors, so that when she moves, all the light in the atmosphere dances for her. I long for such clothing.

They see me too, for someone lifts her arm and waves without a sound. There is a village still sleeping, I remember. When they reach me, we greet one another. The girl with the mirrors is Uvakai, and her younger sister is Eeranila.

'Singing pleases the goddess,' Animalar says. 'Most of the ritual is only that. But first, we must bathe. I'm so glad you could come, Kodhai.'

Without reserve, the sisters begin to unwind their clothing. Animalar takes and tosses each in turn over the branches of a low tree, so they hang like curtains. Eeranila's pavadai-davani shimmers, the mirrors revealing light as though capturing secrets. She has not yet adapted to the sari, despite having been dressed in it at her menarche ceremony in the weeks before. Animalar notes both these things, and lightly admonishes her. From tomorrow, she must wear a full sari, plain in form.

Uvakai and Eeranila run into the lake, each with a hand over her mouth so as not to – I realize why as soon as they plunge in – shout upon being engulfed by the chill. Animalar adjusts the length of her own sari on the branch and turns to me. She hesitates for a moment, but doesn't press. She too, as long-bodied as a man and as thin as a grain stalk, runs into the lake. She enters it without a sound.

Unused to all of this, I had already bathed. I am caught between the embarrassment of letting this on and wanting to do this sincerely, but I have also never bathed with even my breasts bare. But I know it is equally ridiculous to knot my sari under my armpits. So I finally wade into the water behind her, my crisp fresh sari wrinkling and absorbing weight.

This is the first time I have ever been inside a body of water.

It is like everything I had carried all my life has lost its gravity. The one moment of terror I feel when there is nothing but the lake above or below or around me dissolves as soon as my toes touch the bed of silt at its bottom. And then I feel absolutely, and without parallel, free.

It is colder to come out of the lake than to be inside it. The air hits my skin, makes my teeth chatter. The others knot their dry saris around their waists tightly, using the shapes of their bodies as a girdle. I have nothing to wear. I stand dripping, unable to not stare at their bodies, and their ease in their own skins. 'Wait,' Animalar instructs. I wait. She disappears in the direction of their homes, and returns some minutes later with a thin cotton sari. I have never – not even in the grove at midnight – been completely naked in the outdoors, within sight of anyone.

If I go behind the tree, my fellow covenant-keepers will not see me, but who might? Who knows what eyes have followed us girls down these paths, have watched us immerse ourselves in the lake?

'Quickly, please,' says Animalar. She turns to the sisters and asks Eeranila to go and bring from the stoop of her house the tray that contains a clay lamp, wicks, tinder and oil. Uvakai is to follow her and fill the rest of the tray with fresh white jasmine, plucked from the bushes by her house.

I stand there soaked through and with no choice but to walk this defeat back to my father's house, where I will weep by the well and never sit on the stoop as the cowherds come home again, or to do as they just have. I close my own eyes and undress, the cold hitting me in a way that makes me shiver and feel sensuous at once – this I had not known, that hoarfrost can bring pleasure like heat does. I don't linger though. I throw the loose end of the sari over my breasts and left shoulder and knot the long fabric around my waist as the others have done. With this semblance of modesty, I pleat the yards in between and tuck it in at the crotch.

Thus dried and dressed, we sit on the banks of the lake. Animalar loosens a tiny cylinder of vermillion powder from the knot at the end of her sari, and we dot our bare foreheads with it. For the month to come, we are forbidden from darkening our eyelids or wearing flowers in our hair. But a bare forehead is inauspicious.

And then, with our own hands, in that piercing and electrically beautiful winter morning, we fill our palms with sand and invoke the goddess. We mould her body from the earth, and line crevices for the features of her face using the fingertips of our smallest fingers. And finally, Animalar opens the cylinder of vermillion and asks me to dot the goddess's forehead.

And there, on the banks of the lake in which we purified ourselves for her, on the banks from which we shaped her from mud and made her manifest before us, we bow and pray to the goddess Katyayani. In whose name we make this vow that will change the tides of our lives, through which the divine must now move like lunar pull on water.

On the night that follows – the first night of Margali – the planets Sukran and Guru linger in the night sky along with that gravid moon that had watched me walk from my well to the wide embrace of the lake that morning. I watch them, glimmering in the early darkness, just as I am. The afterglow of having commenced my vow radiates through me. I am alone at the back of the house, beyond the kitchen, near the cowshed from which come occasional sounds of lowing, sleep descending on the animals after a day in the fields. Once again, the first night on which my eyes opened to the heavens above Vishnuchittan's grove of tulasi palpitates my memory like a raindrop in well water.

Tonight, under this arena of starlight, I take up my stylus and press it by the glow of a clay lantern into dry palmyra leaves. It is on this night that I dedicate myself – to my *self*, to who I truly am, to what is invincible and without bondage of time, that predates me, that will outlive me. I travel as I write, wayfaring on the hallucinogenic of words, the act of their scripting a form of magic that makes me forget all else than where they take me – which is also the place from where they came. And in this way I enter the landscape of Ayarpadi, distant in space and time, where the people of the cows roam the forest and enter its rivers every day. I am among its girls, among its women, and we are prosperous for among us is the fierce prince, the lion cub who had been raised by Yashoda of the beauteous eyes. His own eyes are lotuses, his body dark like sapphire, his face selenic in radiance, and we want from him a drum, the parai, and we intend to keep our vow until he gives it to us. Through this sacred month of deepest winter, in which the cemmuli bluebell blooms and the nights are long and vivid with wanting, we will ask him and ask again. And the world will rejoice as it listens to our asking. At the end of the leaf-page, I inscribe, without philosophy, the secret words that cannot be translated, that belong to the illiteral inner landscape, that by their repetition bring forth, laud and proliferate.

el-or-empavay.

9

Milk and ghee are also forbidden through this holy month. Supplication requires abstinence. I eat a separate diet from my family. I cook my own meals, coaxing flame and firewood in the kitchen when I come home after my early morning prayer. And again when I eat as evening sets. Through the day, I consume only water and sometimes fruit, relishing the ice apples of the palm tree and the sharpness of raw mango out of season. I am purifying my body and clarifying my mind. I have chosen to isolate myself from the material world by these gestures, to ever remain conscious of my vow, to not think of it only when I wake in the hour of secrets, only to then return unscathed with rheumy eyes into the ordinary.

When I look into the mirror, wearing the lord's garland, I rue how my eyes are less beautiful without their collyrium.

But when the vow has been completed, we will lengthen our eyes like spears. We will kiss beetroots and berries so they stain our lips plush. We will weigh our braids down with crowns of flowers. And a night will come when we ourselves will stain our bridal mats, pierced and pinned by a man's weight. And maybe that night will feel to me like the scratch of rice grain felt when I pressed the first letter of the alphabet into existence. A little pain – and then, the universe.

There is nothing in these rituals that says we cannot dream, for it is desire that makes the world.

10

Padmamma had told me that Nappinai was Radha, Krishna's beloved of beloveds.

But I know what that means, and what it does not. It means that he still had fifteen thousand nine hundred and ninety-nine beloveds, and he belonged to each like fragments of light on broken glass. It means she was not the one he married, although there was another who he did. There is always something disquieted beneath some stories.

It means that I ask Matatilli the same question again the next time I see her, one morning as I walk back from the ritual on the lakeshore. And she tells me that maybe there was a Radha, and she belonged to the dark lord of the Madurai of the north. But there was also a Nappinai, and it was the dark lord who belonged to her.

My grandmother's answer had sufficed to allow me to undertake this vow, for it was within the ways that my family understood. But now, I have more questions.

Matatilli sits on her porch and dries her wet hair as she talks to me. From inside her home, there is the scent of something being brewed. Has she left her stove unattended? The thought breezes into my mind for a second as she speaks.

'Nappinai was a cowherd, a beautiful woman, and to win her hand in marriage Krishna wrestled and defeated seven bulls. She wasn't like his other wives, she wasn't as celestial. She was like me,' – Matatilli grins and reveals a line of teeth like pearls. 'She was like me. She smelt like dung and mud and sweat through most of the day, and at night she smelt like water from a well made fragrant with jasmines, and she was anything but the colour of milk, though she definitely drank a lot of it.'

'Amazing! Tell me more.'

'So, when we pray to the goddess Katyayani to bring us a man like Krishna, we are just like Nappinai. So we must ask for her blessing too. And maybe she *is* Katyayani? And whether Katyayani is the lord's sister or another of his wives, it doesn't matter. But the point is that these women know him. They love him. They know what it is like to be loved by him. And we ask them to share all that love with us, to let us have some of it in our own lives.'

And then a man – tall, wearing a green turban and paying very little attention to me – comes out of her house, carrying two terracotta cups in his hands, and he gives one to her and one to me and then he disappears – and for a brief moment a sunset pinkness flashes over Matatilli's round cheekbones.

'Drink it,' she says. 'It's good for you. It's milk boiled with thippili, dried ginger and some leaves.'

I lift the cup to my lips, steam rising, but don't sip yet.

'Chi,' she admonishes me. 'Don't look so excited, child. He is only passing through. In two days he'll be gone, with his wares and his mountain herbs.'

'I didn't know there was a man in your life.'

She laughs. 'There isn't one.'

'There are many?'

'Child...'

All of this is so new to me. I thought such things only existed in the great poems, not in our small modern town with its many rules and its unvaried days.

'Now,' she says, swallowing a large sip of her drink. 'You be good, complete the pavai nombu. Find yourself a husband, because that is what you want. But first finish your drink and go home, your father is waiting for you. I'll see you later when I come to work.'

We have just begun to pat water into the sand on the banks of the lake, to shape our goddess of the clear morning, when it suddenly strikes us that Matatilli should be with us. Shameless, sweet-talking Matatilli, older than us all, wise in ways we envy and long to be. At first, Animalar refuses to interrupt our prayers, but when she sends Eeranila to bring our offerings of fresh flowers, she concedes to allowing a quick rap on the front door – just to see if she will wake, our teacher, our trailblazer, whose hips curve like a cobra's hood, and whose lovely hands are always red from milking.

Eeranila returns without her, bringing only a tray laden with jasmines – and fresh lilies from the pond behind Matatilli's house.

I see this pond for myself on the mornings that follow when I arrive even earlier than usual, to try to rouse Matatilli so that she too can participate in the pavai nombu. So that she too can have what we all seek, whether we admit it or otherwise – and so that she, knowing more than us all, can help guide the lord (for surely he too has admired her breasts, and the long thick plait of hair that hangs to her bottom like a rope-bucket in a well) onto the dirt path that leads to us, bathing in chilly water, praying each time that he will have come and stolen our clothing so that we must emerge from the lake as pure as the days we were born.

But she does not wake.

I invent rituals: I call out to her and say 'Precious one, please give us the fan! Cherished one, please give us the mirror!' She does not respond. '*Lovely one!*' I shout. 'Let him go, you have kept him to yourself, smothered him in only your musk. Share him with us, and we'll share you with him.'

And each morning she refrains, but when we have finished our prayers, when our hibiscus-eared goddess has been left to sit in the sand into which she will slowly merge again during the course of the day, Matatilli is often by her front porch. Her large eyes freshly lined, her hair wet, and her face always adorned with a smile.

And so when I write of Nappinnai, when I dedicate these poems to her and entreat her to come to us with our lord, it is Matatilli I think of, who would not wake. Who refused to show us her face no matter how sharply we knocked or how loudly we called, who would not step out of her bedroom to be a part of this precious vow. And who would not tell us why.

11

On the evening of the new moon, a storm gathers over the mountain range, darkening clouds heaving across the skies until they arrive and burst over Puduvai, and drench us with a pleasure like the monsoon gives, here in the brittleness of deep winter.

We have prayed for this rain. We have prayed also for fields so fertile that carp swim between the stalks of tall red paddy, and for an all-prevalent peace that allows even restless beetles to sleep placidly within the dewy petals of blue water lilies, and for the udders of our cows to be so heavy with milk that our hands cannot keep up with their flow, and that the milk nourishes the earth too as rain does the rivers. We have prayed to be safeguarded and free of all evil. We have prayed, most of all, for love.

Let love come to me as clouds have come over the mountains. Let it fill me like rainwater fills the hollows of monkey cup flowers. Let it burden me like yellow blossoms burden summer-kissed laburnum trees. Let it emerge into view – a subtle brightening – the way Sukran rose in the early twilight just as Guru was setting on the first night of my vow. We are midway deep. From here on, we are closer to completion than to the initiation.

Let it bring me Vishnu himself, for no mortal man can match me, no one can claim Kodhai of Puduvai the way an artless man will keep his fortune-telling parrot within bars, robbing the bird of its powers by exerting control over it. I will never be so clipped. I will never be so conquered.

It is this conviction that keeps me company as I sit on the stoop at the back of our house, willing the moment of inspiration to strike so that I can begin writing my poem for the day. And then I see Animalar running up the path, her expression so cheerful that she cannot possibly have any other news but the one she brings. I recognize it on her face from many feet away and something ugly pangs in me, makes me forget to rearrange my own.

12

Each morning – or more accurately, deep, deep into each night – we wake and bathe in water that chills us to our bones, dress ourselves simply and raise from the earth a goddess made manifest by desire, word and touch, our fingers in the mud that makes her body, dotting her third eye without drawing our own two. In our hearts we hold the world: we hold the fields and their rains, the valleys and their villagers. We hold the flute song of the playful one as the tune by which we suffer our days without ghee or milk, and the nights when the stars burst open like seed pods above the groves and gardens we surrender to. We want everything we can name. By deep night and by new day, by waning moon and waxing womb-fire, we ask. We ask. We ask.

And to the goddess we pray, to become her. To be so immaculate. To be so adored.

And when my prayer ends, in the still silent space before the world wakes, or sometimes in the hours before it begins, I sit with my lantern in the cowshed, which faces neither large roads nor curious windows, and I write. I say the words under my breath over and over and commit them to memory even as I press the tip of my stylus into my book of bound palm leaves, writing, writing, writing. If something were to happen to my manuscripts, my poems will remain housed within my body, nestled in the pounding of my blood.

By the first light of morning, I join my father as he goes into the grove to pluck the materials for the day's garland. And then we sit together and weave it as the sky mellows to the colour of hyacinth dye. And finally, I place the fresh garland on my shoulders and smile at myself in the mirror, and walk with him to the temple – the weight of my love cascading in flower and leaf, caressing my high and tender breasts.

13

As the month of Margali nears its end, I finally ask Matatilli why the pavai nombu had not worked for her. What I had meant to ask was why she had not tried it again, in the years since the death of her first love, but the question came out wrong. And I was wrong to assume in any case. Matatilli's betrothed had come into her life without preamble or petition. They had grown up together, among the cows, and fallen in love. She had owned that preciousness before she could ever yearn for it, and then it was taken from her.

She tells me this, then looks at me seriously and says, 'I tried for two years, consecutively. The year after I turned twenty-two. The year after I turned twenty-three. Nothing came for me. I could not will it into being.'

'The vow can fail then,' I say flatly. This was what I had feared and suspected. My belly churns. I will not be permitted even a year, after which to try again. By the next winter, I would be somebody's wife. I would live under his roof, boiling hot water for his parents and learning how to not cry out when he beats me. In the worst of moods, someone would call me an illegitimate child, or a prostitute – that word used by those who do not believe a woman owns her own body, or her own self – and, inevitably, of unknown and therefore untouchable caste – that concept for those who believe God ordains their superiority at the expense of all humanity. I know it, I know it, I know it. My heart is speared by this knowing. My father would sell his grove for my bride wealth. My mother would learn to prostrate at the feet of my in-laws, so they would be kinder to me. My grandmother would never be told what was truly happening to me, so as to protect her heart. I would learn to lie whenever I visited her, to hold my clothing over my bruises just so.

Our neighbour's daughter who had come of age just a little before I did had accepted exactly this fate. She had been married when she was little, and finally moved into her new home. Pregnant within weeks, her husband spat suspicions at her and threatened at the mildest displeasure to send her back to her parents, with the implicit danger that they too would turn her out. Unskilled beyond the demands of the hearth, it would only be her body that would feed her. So this girl, almost but not even my age, keeps her mouth shut and massages her mother-in-law's back day after day, probably keeps her mouth shut as her husband violates her night after night, and certainly keeps her mouth shut even when that god-fearing family she married into sing together in the temple. I have seen her mouth as thin as a line in the sand, her hand over her belly almost a fist. She will probably keep her mouth shut even as baby after baby tears out into the world from her.

I know it, I know it, I know it. No matter how much Vishnuchittan wants the world to be god-lit, it will remain precisely as wretched as it is, and so he will sell my freedom in order to buy my security. And he will regret it.

My father – maker of garlands, receiver of visions, the one who showed me how to see into all the worlds before and beyond – will stand with slumped shoulders like every man at the house of his daughter's in-laws, waiting for word to be given so that he can cross the threshold. And he will say nothing, for these are the laws of this world. I would rather die than let this happen.

That evening, as I lay the plantain leaves on the ground for the last meal of the day, I ask Vishnuchittan quietly if we could spend some time with our books after we eat. He agrees. Amma stands beside me with a bowl of rice, which she scoops with a smaller vessel, then places neat mounds on the leaves. I bring the ghee, which I myself cannot partake, and pour it lightly over the rice. Amma and I take turns. She brings the gravy, steaming hot, and I bring the cool yoghurt. A small flask of jaggery-sweetened milk waits for the meal's end. Tastes I have not had in weeks. My own meal consists of steamed millet that I eat with shredded coconut and a pinch of jaggery. We all eat together; even Padmamma joins us, sitting on a new stool, with a small table that had been carpentered just for her because of her legs. Still, out of long custom that had simply ossified into habit, my father, as always, is served first.

After dinner, I help Padmamma outdoors for her ablutions and then back to her mat to sleep, and when I am sure she's no longer listening, I go to Vishnuchittan's corner of the house, stacked floor to ceiling with bound manuscripts. He has been reading as he waited for me, or so it seems until he glances up and squints. It is too dark to read, and his eyes are getting older. But I have to ask him.

'What is it?' he asks me first.

'Tonight is the twenty-seventh night. My vow is nearly complete.'

'It is not complete yet. You should not raise doubts this early.'

How had he known? He raises his palm to hush my protest.

'Everyone around you marvels at your faith, and how far you have come,' he goes on.

I begin to cry. Is there nothing that will let me be heard?

'Animalar was engaged in two weeks!'

'Animalar knew what she wanted, and she wanted something that she could have. What do you want, Kodhai? Is it something you can have?'

'How can you ask me this? You know what I want.'

'Kodhai, kannamma, the lord lives eternally within your heart. But you live here in this world. Be a part of it, my child. Don't break my heart.'

'You are asking me to be unfaithful.' My face burns to say these words to my father.

'God doesn't see in such absolutes. Those are the ideas of men.'

'I will belong to no one but him.'

'You frighten me, child. Please.'

'You—' I spit out. 'I never expected this from you.'

My father opens the book in his lap, its leaves held together by twine looped through a small, cleanly-cut aperture. He pretends to look through it, but his eyes are withdrawn. I know he is thinking deeply. I look out of the window and see the moon nearly rounded into fullness. It had been full on the day when I began my vow. It will be full on the day that it ends.

'What do the scriptures say about this vow I am keeping?' I ask finally.

Vishnuchittan closes the manuscript before him as though accepting its futility and looks straight at me. Even in the darkness, I see how my father's jowls have begun to sag, how silver now shoots through his eyebrows and hair. 'Long before you were born, I fought your grandfather, who trained priests. I fought him when he said that the gods know only one language, and that this language in turn should be spoken or heard only by our caste. By the *men* of our caste, that is. I fought him when he said the written word is more precious than the voice. So, to you, my daughter, I say: perhaps one day the vow you undertook will be scripture too. But for now, it is mainly song. I gave you my consent to undertake the pavai nombu. But assurance was never mine to give you.'

'I have decided I will not marry.'

'Then will you terminate this vow? Or will you terminate your –,' he sputters, then sighs.

'I will not terminate my vow. I will complete it. But it is not enough.'

'Then what comes next?'

'Take me to see Anuman Acharya.'

My father draws his breath in. 'No.'

'This is what I want.'

'You are too young for this. This can never happen. And understand something: there are no paths for the woman who does not belong to a household.'

I look at my father, who told his father that there are no lines on earth not drawn by man, who tells me now that those lines must not be crossed anyway. I cannot speak because of my tears.

'I must go to Madurai to celebrate Pongal at Raja Srimara Srivallabha's court,' he then says. 'I have been invited especially this year. Please, my child, come with me. See that there is a world beyond Puduvai. See that there are other ways to live.' Tears wet his own cheeks. He shudders. 'This is my fault. This is my fault! I should have given you more than this. I should not have let you become like me.'

'Like you?' He is not like me. No.

'Please come to Madurai. I pray for only one more thing in this life. May the lord come into your life as love, just as you seek, but let there be someone…'

'Is Amma then Maha Vishnu, for you?'

'No, kanna,' he says, and wipes his eyes before he looks at me again. 'You are.'

14

That night, I write about sweet offerings of food, satisfaction, celebration. We have begun to adorn ourselves again, in the psychic landscape that I enter in my poetry, that distant land known as Ayarpadi, where every cowherd is decked with gold. Even in these visions I wear my conch bangles, and they turn wet with the ghee that drips all the way to my elbows, for so rich is the feast we have made and partake in. We have received the parai, the precious drum that keeps the rhythm of the cosmos. We have conquered his heart. But somehow it is still not enough for me. And when I have finished writing, I do not go into the grove. Instead I sit on the step at the back of the house and watch tiny fires burning in the distance, and wonder what they are. Who had set them alight? Each night, something that can neither be quenched nor extinguished scorches me from within. It is more than the pleasure my body seeks, the pleasure my hands fulfil in the absence of a lover. Life is at once material and illusory. And living itself is not enough.

And in the morning, when my father leaves for the temple, carrying the garland I have worn, I sit by myself on the thinnai and watch the birds that burdened the tamarind trees' branches all night take flight. And then I get up and start walking down the path, in the opposite direction, until I arrive just beyond the priestly quarter. At the house of Anuman Acharya, the most ascetic of all of Puduvai's priests, I wipe my feet on the grass outside his compound and go and sit on his thinnai, resting my back on a pillar, facing inwards in the hope that no one will see me from the street. I do not know if I should call out, and so I wait. It is not long before a very elderly woman comes out slowly, carrying a small earthen vessel. The skin around the gems in her nose and ears droop from years of weight. She seems frail in every conceivable way. I stand up quickly to take her arm but she bristles. Of course. She does not know who I am – or more accurately, who I am from. 'I am the daughter of Vishnuchittan, beneficiary of Raja Srimara Srivallabha, granddaughter of Mukund Acharya of the four Vedas,' I announce.

She appraises me. 'What is your name and what do you want?'

'My name is Kodhai and I must speak to the Acharya as I complete my vow, which I have kept through Margali, in praise of our lord.'

She allows me inside. The house smells of burning grasses, and something hums within it, something I have felt far within the forest of magnolias, in the caverns behind waterfalls, and sometimes in certain temples at certain moments.

The Acharya knows who I am even though his mother did not, and he listens as I tell him everything. His questions are but few. And then he agrees to what I ask of him.

For the first time in my life, I let the bodice of my sari slip before a man. He does not look at me as I do this, as I bring the loose end flat across my back and pull it tight over my chest. My throat is bare even of gold, for the thin necklace I have worn since my menarche ceremony is what I have given this man as my tithe to take this initiation. My arms are bare. My shoulders are bare. I shiver from fear and coldness, from desperation and exhilaration. And when he takes a tiny flame to a long blade of sturdy grass, I retreat into my mind. If I scream, I do not hear it. I enter the forest, roaming with my cows. I love my lord as artlessly as a child. He who was born in my clan of little understanding but profound blessing has forgiven me, has let me solder my sins in him. And now the bond between us can never be broken. My eyes stay closed, even if my teeth clench, even if my mouth opens. And when I return from my trance, the conch adorns my left shoulder and the discus my right. And the silver seals that emblazoned them onto my skin lie on either side of my Acharya, and somewhere near him are embers still uncooled, still fiercely glowing. It is only my heart that is as placid as a body of still water after the rains, holding fresh knowledge in its bosom, overwhelmed by the end of the drought.

And when the garland is next brought to me for the rite of adoration, it is consecrated by my shoulders which bear the brand of the lord, that bare for all to see that I belong only and ultimately to him.

15

Margali ends, and I complete a manuscript of thirty poems on the morning after the last ritual on the lakeshore, when we have raised and given praise to a goddess made of earth for the final time. I write the concluding poem with my back to a tree by that same lake as dry winter leaves drift to me occasionally from its boughs. From tomorrow, ghee and milk are ours again, as are painted eyes and blossom-braided hair. Tomorrow is the first day of Pongal, the festival of the harvest. I walk home by the dawnlight. When I return, my father hastens to have me wear Vatapatrasayi's garland so that we can leave for Madurai, where those who have received patronage like him have been invited to participate in this year's milk boiling ceremony at the royal court. In the compound, a bullock swishes its tail, around which flies cluster mercilessly. It is yoked to a cart, and a driver wearing a shawl with the fish emblem sits upfront. Vishnuchittan wants us to have a good night's rest in the city, instead of arriving dishevelled from travel tomorrow morning.

I have never been to Madurai. I have never been further than Shenbaga Thoppu. The truth is that I have also rarely been on a bullock cart, for my feet have taken me wherever I've been, and my inner eye has taken me even further.

The dirt road to the city curves and swerves and curves again, although the land is flat, for it follows a natural logic of growth, cutting through rather than alongside the fields. In the first two hours alone I recognize mustard, many types of millets, maize and innumerable trees, neither pod nor fruit prolific at this time of year. I intend to stay awake through this journey, to see everything. The mountains rise in the distance to our left. When we pass through villages and towns, plumes of smoke often surround us, for it is the day of Bhogi, when every household is engaged in a ritual of renewal, cleansing all its corners with smoke, burning all the things that are no longer needed. In order to ask for more, as we will tomorrow on the second and most important day of Pongal, we must first be willing to give up what is not meant for us.

The bullock cart carries only my father and I in its back, because there is no one else from Puduvai who has been invited to this celebration. It stops once, somewhere midway, to allow us all to relieve ourselves in the bushes. It's an odd thrill when I squat and loosen my bladder. I wish I had known this was permissible. I wish I hadn't always run home from places all over town, afraid to lift my sari anywhere but in our shed; I hadn't even ever relieved myself inside the lake. How strange it is that everything man builds, he builds to forget the body, but everything in nature is so harmonious with it. Imagine if we simply went into nature and allowed her to absorb our waste into mulch. Perhaps then humans wouldn't have to suffer the indignity of carrying others' night soil on their heads, without their shadows ever darkening the thresholds of those who made the rules.

We arrive in Madurai in the late afternoon, hungry and hoping for rest. But the city, with its arresting colours and imposing monuments, sweeps me into its thrall immediately. I forget everything for some time, all my pinings and my frustrations. It is so wonderful just to be here. To walk streets studded with shops that sell things I didn't know I wanted until I saw them – painted sticks that swirl in ebullient colours when hung in the wind, toys that rattle when shaken, fragrant oils in tiny bottles that smell like gardens, and of sweet foreign beans and petrichor. To look at buildings that stand three floors tall, with so many windows, and balconies where women bend over as though unaware their décolletage is being revealed, as flowering creepers climb the metal railings as though they were shoots of cane. We are ushered into rooms decorated with fabrics so beautiful and expensive that my friends and I, or even my mother and I, would never think to drape them on our bodies, let alone cover our pillows with them.

I have not been invited to an audience with the king, which my father will enjoy tomorrow, but that night we are both asked to a special feast for all the royal guests. I dress in one of my two good saris, bought especially for this trip. It is soft pink with white embroidery, and I buy jasmine for my hair, so famously fragrant in this city, but add a sprig of davanam to decorate it too. I don't want to look like all the other women, I decide. But when I enter the long hall, lined on either side with plantain leaves for the feast, I am disappointed to see that I am the only woman. The men all seem to stare at me and also not see me at all.

To my father's other side sits a man with a shaven head, wearing a string of rudraksha seeds like a circlet around his forehead. He wears them also on his wrists and upper arms, and looped loosely thrice around his throat so they form three necklaces. In various parts of his body are smeared three fingers of white ash, and between his brows is a small round dot of vermillion. Like everyone else on this side of the hall, he wears the priestly crossbelt. He introduces himself to Vishnuchittan only as Vadhavoorar, a man from the town of Vadhavoor, and does not offer another name. They greet one another, then the other man casts a curious look at me.

'My daughter Kodhai, here,' Vishnuchittan says, 'has begun to write poems too. Over Margali, she composed a poem for each day. I found them very beautiful. One day you must come to Puduvai and hear her sing in the temple.'

I have neither shared my poems with my father nor sung them in the temple yet, but he has heard them no doubt, as I composed them. I am joyous.

'It would be my honour,' says Vadhavoorar. And then he does something that takes me entirely by surprise, for I have never seen men address young women in the company of their guardians. He leans back and catches my eyes and says to me directly, 'It is my pleasure to meet you, Ammaiyar. In whose praise do you sing?'

I find my voice. 'In praise of Maha Vishnu, Iyah. Like my father.'

'I see. I too have been writing through Margali, in praise of my lord, the crescent-crowned one, Sivaperuman. I was in Thiruvannamalai until last night, singing to him. Twenty verses, one for each lady who was doing penance there, keeping the pavai nombu.'

I start. 'I have just kept the pavai nombu!'

My father shoots a look at me, as though I have revealed something too personal. But I don't care. I am so delighted to know that the rituals we have held in our small-town matter in the wider world.

'Wonderful!' says Vadhavoorar. 'May all you wish be willed into being. And your poems – may they ever be sung.' He turns to Vishnuchittan. 'Blessed are you, oh Leader of the Learned, for a daughter who may tower over you as the temple gopuram towers over even the deity.'

'You haven't heard or read my poems,' I say. I am not so easily swayed.

'I will,' he says, and bends towards his leaf and his meal. 'I am sure of it.'

16

The next morning is the first one in a month in which I have not risen in the depths of the night to bathe in the cold lake water and pray. But it is the first day of the month of Thai, and the second day of the festival of Pongal, when everywhere that the Tamil language resounds the sun is praised for the bounty of the harvest to come. So I still wake early, and wear my new parrot-green sari with red mangoes embroidered along the borders, and while Vishnuchittan goes to the royal court for the ceremonial milk-boiling, I make my way through the vibrant streets of Madurai, drawn to and through them as if by instinct. When the cloying, grassy smell of cow dung hits me as I turn a corner, I know I have found my destination.

Here, I unwrap the drape of my saree so that it no longer covers my arms. My shoulders are bare, and I am proud to show off my new tattoos, even if they still feel slightly raw to the touch. I know that in these quarters, no one will look at me only to admire my limbs, for every woman here moves more freely than she does elsewhere, fabric thrown over the breasts and only one shoulder, her entire clavicle exposed on her right side. She can hike her sari up. She can jump. She can run far, far away…

Someone grabs my hands and spins me and suddenly I am in the middle of a circle and the only way to not fall down is to keep moving. I imitate the person opposite me – the way she claps her hands and sways her arms, the way she wiggles everywhere just a little so her whole body seems like a ball finding its balance. I'm dancing! Before I know it, I'm laughing and whirling like I've never not known how to do this.

Around me are many other spinning circles, each composed of girls and women breathlessly, exuberantly, moving to the sounds of many drums. A woman with a loud, strong voice starts singing, and the dancers respond in chorus. I keep up as well as I can. And when the chorus shouts 'Govinda!' I call out with all my heart.

And then the drum beats cease and every dancer drops to the ground and sits. I can feel my pulse throbbing all over my legs. The woman who sang now begins to recite the Tamil names of Maha Vishnu, and after each one we should out 'Potri!'. Victory be to he of sapphire skin, who spanned all three worlds with three steps, who will dissolve the universe when its time has come.

And then she begins to tell a story, in a lilting meter. There are seven bulls in the stable, and seven daughters in the seven houses that surround it. There are seven notes in the musical scale, and seven lifetimes over which one is reborn to find and lose and love again the partner of their soul and body. There are seven women and girls in each circle here, and each of them has a place in this dance of joy that unites Krishna with his consort, the Lady of the Cowherds, our own petal-lipped, bell-hipped Nappinai.

O Katyayani, O Kamadeva, I think, *maybe you have heard me after all.*

I see now that in each circle is one woman who wears a peacock feather in her hair, tucked high into a bun on top of her head. She is the one who will play Krishna in this dance, and the one who stands to her left is Krishna's brother Balarama. And to Balarama's left is Nappinai.

I have cavorted like a calf into this circle, invited by chance, not knowing that all along I was dancing in the place of Nappinai.

I wish Animalar, Eeranila and Uvakai – and Matatilli, most of all – could have been here to share this moment with me. I cannot wait to tell them what is happening.

Together, we sing of how Krishna seduced Nappinnai in the waters of the Yamuna, and we sing of how he stole her bangles and hid her clothes, and we sing of how in the end it was she who ruled, for among all goods and tenures she had captured his heart.

And we sway and clap, and sway and clap, and exclaim 'Govinda!' and exclaim 'Gopala!', and we spin and we spin until we have no sense of orientation and nothing exists but this epiphanic joy. The song crescendos and nadaswarams begin to blare alongside the percussion. And suddenly there's a garland of jasmines in my hands and I know I'm supposed to throw it over the neck of the peacock-crowned woman, and she spins me to her bosom and in that moment, I am hers.

And just then, from the open firewood stoves in the near distance rises another excitation. The milk pots have begun to boil over, each within seconds of the one before it, and the milk pours over terracotta cambers into the earth. It is the most auspicious sign that good will prevail in this land and amongst the crops, along the rivers and in the coffers of king and country. And when the grains and jaggery inside the pots have cooked, rice browned to lusciousness will be distributed so that every tongue in this land will taste sweetness on this blessed day, and take that blessing to the threshing floor and to the winnowing fans, to the kitchen's heat and to the granary.

'Pongal-o-Pongal!' the crowd jubilates.

When the sweet pongal is distributed, I place just one grain on my tongue for the sake of ritual. I cannot eat, for I have decided to fast, consuming only one meal every day. If I eat this early in the morning, I am sure that by evening I will not be able to stand. The somnolent hours of the late afternoon will be the best time to eat. But having been deprived of milk for a month, I drink it with greed. I ask if I can milk a cow by myself, angle its thick teats into a small mud cup someone has lent me, and drink and drink my fill, and breathe a kiss into the animal's mud-streaked hide when I am done.

I am curious, exhilarated with everything that this morning and this big city have contained. I truly feel as if I am in Ayarpadi, as if I have no other identity, and all my seven lifetimes can pass in this pleasure.

Beyond the cowshed is a stable where the looming shapes of bullocks move. I walk closer and observe them.

I have never seen bulls like these before, only deeply domesticated ones, the aggression taken out of them with comfort and regular mating. But even tied to their posts, these bulls emanate an entirely disturbing energy. It draws me in even as it makes the hair on my arms stand. Muscle and vein throb beneath their taut hides, the undulating curve of each large dark hump nearly obscene in its definition. The bulls stand taller than I am, their horns so proudly erect it is like they have pierced the air. The air itself: virile, earthy, desirous, untrustable. When one of them lets out a bellow, a shiver runs through me that makes me not know whether I want to remain rooted to the ground and watch what happens next, or if I want to run.

17

That afternoon, my father accompanies me to a place a few hours north of the towers of Madurai, where in the lowest slopes of the densely-thicketed mountain of Thirumaliruncholai is a temple to Vishnu in a form so exquisite that his name itself is Beautiful One. We cross the Cilampu, an anklet of a stream, a tributary of the great gushing Vaigai, before we arrive at the foothills. Behind us follow eight more carts, paid for with a part of my bride wealth, but which I have promised to earn my keep for, somehow. Vishnuchittan's face is in shadow through the journey.

At this temple, I offer the one hundred pots of butter and one hundred pots of rice the bullock carts have carried to tempt and persuade my lord. And I stand before the beautiful one whose shoulders were made for my repose with my nipples tender and stiff like jasmine buds, and promise him a hundred thousand pots more to come if only he will come to me, if he will enter me and smear the saffron paste that I pressed to my breasts, imagining his own four hands.

And so, I begin anew on the day when the first harvest is celebrated. I begin again what failed the first time, and hone my entreaty down to its sharpest and most selfish focus. If I pray for rain it is for womanly wetness. If I pray for the weight of udders, it is for my swelling breasts to be held and fondled. If I pray for frolicking carp or lush yield, it is only for play and pleasure. With him. For me, for me, for me.

These are secret rites but they require of me exposure that will not keep them so. I'm accessing what came to me in dreams. I'm making them up as I go along.

Here, I begin. Here, in the wild peacock-gilded temenos of Thirumaliruncholai, where in the slopes far above me war elephants – abundant in the armoury that the god Murugan made of the bower where his beloved Valli, woman dark as a mango leaf, reigned and played – roam untethered in times of peace, and down below are cool ponds filled with lotuses as lovely as my Narayana's eyes, I begin. I draw mandalas of rice powder before this distant shrine to Kamadeva, its short pillars overrun with creepers full of laughing flowers, and paint the inner walls of the sanctum with secret diagrams and syllables that run together and reveal all of my longing when intoned. I draw his banner, with its motifs of a shark, attendants carrying fly-whisks and his bow of black sugarcane. I dip my fingers into a pot of wet flour and use them like fine brushes. In the groves of the hill, still brittle and waiting for spring, I find thornless twigs and conflagrate them. On this, I cook newly harvested grain, and offer these to him along with raw paddy, sugar cane and rice sweetened with jaggery. I pluck the dangerous datura flower, petals closed – for it is a vespertine – and sweet-scented marjoram leaves, and offer these at his feet. I am beseeching him directly. No mediators can speak for me any longer for I have crossed into a spectral place. I have been denied what should come to all in the material world, and I want to transcend it. But I also want its deepest ecstasy. I do not know how else I will survive.

I stand before him and unfurl my heart like a flag, and I sing.

I will keep this vow until something breaks.

18

Here is one thing that happens, or never does.

When I have completed my rite to Kamadeva, I walk down the great hill of Thirumaliruncholai, past the snake-mounds of the goddess in its upper reaches and her waterfall, past the great monument to Vishnu, the beautiful one, who has eaten all my butter and all my rice but not yet satisfied me, past the shrine to the black, billhook-wielding guardian deity Karuppannaswamy, whose sandalwood-smeared altar doors must remain closed for all but one day of the year, and I keep walking until I arrive by myself to the banks of the Cilampu. My father has left me with a single bullock cart to find my way back to Madurai. My heart had felt pinched when he had told me this earlier, for the freedom I had sought and won also meant that he had given up on me in some way, that between us was a gap quarried by my actions. The bullock cart waits for me at the temple, and I had walked past it too. I want to rest for a while, for I have yet to break my fast, and will not eat until almost evening. I settle by this beautiful stream that carries in its ripples the essences of black cedar and soothing sandalwood, and wonder if perhaps I can bathe in it, if it may give me succour.

I fall asleep this way. Or I stay awake and build sandcastles by its banks, and undress myself and drape my clothes on tree branches just as my cowherd friends had shown me how to through the disarming, disappointing month that has just passed. I bathe in the river, let sandalwood cool my yearning, slip under the water and touch its murky bed with my feet. When I come up for air, my clothes are gone. And he is standing there, his fists on his hips, smirking at me, threatening to break my sandcastles, and I am suddenly afraid, I am suddenly confused by the entitlement with which he has come here, even though I have given him everything, allowed him to take it all for granted. Where is the line between wanting and violation? What if I had wanted this, but not like *this*? Not so brutally. Not so insouciantly. He takes my wrists in his grip and I swoon – but why?

I wake dishevelled, and when I reach the bullock cart I collapse, and sleep again.

19

But we do not go back to Puduvai that night, as I had thought we would, for my father intends to meet with the king's priests. I know what he is secretly planning. I know that in a few days our local astrologer will come to our house and suggest an array of remedies that may alleviate what we do not know about the houses of my chart. Because we do not know the minute during which I was born, we cannot know which star within the constellation of Simha was in ascendant, and so we cannot know what planets fill my seventh house of marriage, my eighth house of inauspiciousness, or my twelfth house of mystery. All we know is that I am a moon-lion. This augurs some things, and rules out others, but cannot possibly present the whole grid of a birth-chart. With these remedies, and using the prestige of his own fame, my father will try to secure for me a selection of matches. Eligible boys who wear the crossbelt, who have learned the Vedas from their own fathers, who live sequestered from the rest of society and believe God holds them more valuable than everyone else. Vishnuchittan will tell them his daughter of small waist and bright eyes is learned, but not so much as to be challenging, and talented, but not so much as to draw attention to herself. And then, with their own horoscopes in hand, my father who disobeyed his own will ask me not to disobey him.

This inevitability is what I am begging Kamadeva to save me from.

On the third day of Pongal, I leave the royal guesthouse without an escort. First, I feign disinterest in leaving our quarters. Then I wait until Vishnuchittan leaves, and slip out.

Once again, I weave through the humming streets to the cowherds' quarters. And then I see that this is not where the action takes place. Hurriedly, I follow the ones late to rise, the elderly and the unable, the children and their agitated mothers, the women too shy to go with the men. They are all heading in the direction of something that I gather from bits of conversation around me is a great arena. The king and his entourage will be there, I overhear. I am not afraid. If my father spots me in a large crowd, it is simply my destiny to be caught in my small lie.

As we near the arena, the wild percussion coming from its direction becomes louder and louder. There are so many people – Madurai is populous, of course, but it is clear from the mixture of dialects, some hints of confusion and the extreme frisson of excitement in the air that travellers like me have thronged the city for the Pongal celebrations too.

There seem to be many gates into the arena, but the crowd also seems to be diverted into a particular one, and so I simply keep up with the wave as it moves. I notice that there is an intimacy between bodies at such close quarters, coupled with a sort of numbing of one's own sensitivity. A little breathless, a little dazed, I cannot stop to think of whose elbow it is pressing into the pool of sweat in the small of my back. It must surely be the same for the tall woman whose left breast presses into my right cheek as we are shoved and nudged to keep moving, and to the girl to my left whose nose is close to my underarms.

We arrive at last at the bottleneck entrance that allows us into the enclosure, and the arena feels even larger than it seemed to be from the outside. Stacks of long stone bricks form a rectangular fence within, separating us spectators from the spectacle. I begin to shout in excitement along with the crowd. Perhaps the king has arrived? I am not certain. I crane my neck without knowing in which direction to look, and then it becomes clear: a group of young men, bare-bodied but for loincloths and sometimes turbans, are congregated in one corner of the arena. I am close enough to see the narrow mouth of the entrance, decorated with marigold garlands. The men occupy either side of the entrance with their arms in eager positions, their hands restlessly moving at the level of their chests. All their eyes are fixed on the entrance. Within the boundaries that keep the spectators at a distance, sometimes standing on the stone fencing, are musicians bearing tamukku drums held by leather straps over their chests.

The rhythm they strike is trance-like – or perhaps it is just the heat, or my fasting, or the jostle and swarm of so many. I've never experienced anything like this, not even the cowherds' dance of yesterday, and I am thrilled beyond measure.

Suddenly, incomprehensible shouts rise from just beyond sight, and a shudder runs through the young waiting men as though they are all biting back an exclamation upon stubbing the toe.

And then, from the small entrance at which they wait, a bull emerges – big-humped, loftily-horned, its body decorated with bright tasselled fabrics and coloured by pigments. At each end of its horns are small bells, and mirrors stitched into tassels catch the sunlight along its sides. Bells encircle its throat. A large orb of crimson has been painted between its brows. Such a handsome creature, but with such tension in its hooves – and fear in its eyes. It wears a garland of pink chrysanthemums. The first man who reaches for the beast comes away with a handful of petals.

And then the bull runs.

As it runs, the men lunge for it, and have it slip from their grip. All but one, who holds on first by its horns and then with an arm around its hump. He is dragged by the bull's speed like a tattered flag in the wind. Only one person is allowed at a time, someone complains behind me, but this rule is not honoured. And there's something enthralling about watching all the men pounce at once, and watching the bull break free of them all each time.

The man with his arm around the bull's hump loses his grip, and falls to the ground.

But he has won, it seems. All it takes is a certain measure of time before he is declared a winner.

The bull runs free, slowing its pace as it nears a trough filled with grass, then lowers its head and eats. When it shakes its head, all the grandeur it wears shimmers.

The next bull is released, a fiercer one – one so fast that men fall before even touching it. Two young bull-tamers race ahead and grab it at almost the same time, and then it is unclear what they are fighting – the beast or each other. Both drop to the ground within seconds.

I had only heard of this sport, jallikattu, in which bulls are wrestled and tamed each year on the third day of Pongal so that their herders know who among them has the strongest stock for breeding. Men walk away with gold coins and gifts, but the most aggressive and robust of bulls wins something far better – the role of the stud, fed and pampered and polished and asked only to fornicate, unlike his brothers who must also trudge the highways and plough the fields.

I can see now that some of the men are bleeding, tearing strips from their turbans to clot the wounds or tie tourniquets. Others remain resilient, and jump for bull after bull as it is released into the enclosure. Each bull is a pageant onto itself: flower-decked, painted, wearing fabrics and trinkets loud and luminous.

And then I see him, unmistakable – skin like the dense dark wood of the ebony tree, chest and shoulders like some mountain range, a face so radiant that even the brindled moon would retreat in envy of his beauty. His bones glow beneath his skin as he conquers the bull's hump momentarily: cheekbones, clavicle, iliac crest, spine lean and long. His smile could break strung bows. He lifts his eyes and looks right at me and everything in the world that is not him dissolves. It is only for a second, like lightning splitting the sky. And then in the clouds of dust and footfall and powdered dyes, he is gone.

20

Here is another thing that happens, or never does.

In my dream of a thousand elephants, the gods themselves came to my wedding. The streets were decorated in colours so vibrant they would never fade from memory, and on every threshold sat pots of gold, for so thriving was every citizen of the land, and so thrilled were they to participate in this celebration. Beautiful young women lifted these pots above their heads as they danced spontaneously at the sight of the one who was striding towards them, his lovely feet sending tremors of joy and awe through the earth. And through those festive streets, with an army of a thousand flawless elephants surrounding him, strode my Vishnu-Narayana, proud as a young lion, strong as a bull, he himself as majestic as the tuskers he roamed amidst.

I had been dressed in my bridal finery by none other than Katyayani herself. She draped the softest silk around my hips and smiled as she lifted a garland, its mingling scents intoxicating, onto my shoulders. My arms were stacked with orbs of gold, and my fingers and toes were tinged with the reddening paste of maruthani leaves. My eyes and lips were painted dramatically, and from my ears cascaded diamonds. In the bun of hair on one side of my head were peacock plumes. Between my eyebrows, drawn in sandalwood and saffron paste, was the long, flamelike insignia of the lord. My precious parrot sat on one shoulder and nudged my cheek with its wingtips.

A canopy decorated with palm leaves and areca nuts stood at the centre of all these celebrations. Strung along its awnings were bright pearls. Within it, before the ritual fire already lit and encircled by dry grass, were chanting priests summoning the aegis of the one who had already promised me everything.

He entered the bridal canopy to the resonances of loud drums and sonorous conches. He took my hand in his and stood beside me, and beside him I scintillated and swerved, flowered and overflowed.

In this dream, I had family that extended by many branches – I had brothers, and belonged by blood to a king. Together with the gods, my relatives kindled the ritual fire, their faces bright with joy and flushed with heat, and rejoiced in my marriage.

Sages and seers joined the priests, dipping mango leaves into pots of sanctified water and scattering their droplets in every direction. They chanted more sacred verses still, for the divine loves poetry, ever adores intonations reverberating through time and space, rendering even the most ordinary of all things sublime.

They took threads smeared with turmeric and tied them around our wrists, my groom's and mine. And then my love knelt and took each of my feet with his beautiful hands and placed it on the grinding stone, and slipped nuptial rings on the second toes.

Drenched with the scents and colours of sandalwood and vermillion, we mounted one of his mighty elephants and paraded through the streets. The elated people, dancing, singing the praises of our perfect union, sprayed rosewater into the heavens. And like this we were joined in eternal conjugal bliss.

But when I wake, it is to the rhythm of the wheels of the cart beneath my back, their lurch and roll over stones and sticks and flattened blades of grass. I sit up and see my father sitting at the back of the cart, facing the miles we have already covered, a distance in his eyes like I have seen some mornings as he weaves his garland, and I feel farther from him than I ever have before.

21

Things have changed. I can see it upon our return to Puduvai. It is only when I notice the disenchanted faces of Padmamma and Amma that I realize I had expected to be welcomed back with pomp. For who among the women and girls of this town has been to Madurai, has slept on the satin-covered pillows of Raja Srimara Srivallabha's guesthouse, or of any king before him, and met with luminaries from all over the Pandya kingdom, even if only to be introduced as the poet's daughter?

But that is not to be. I can see that my family no longer knows how to be with me, and I am losing touch with what it means to have a family contain me. I know that this family – my family – was a gift, for if it was not for them I would have been an orphan. And no matter who else raised me, I would not have been given the key to the scriptures, and to the alphabet that forms them line by line. But nothing has been the same since I walked through that front door with my shoulders burning, the conch and discus inseparable from my body. I can sense that no one knows with ease anymore what the right thing to do with me is.

Only I know what I must do. And now I also know no one can stop me, or should even dare try.

Because my father will not allow me to travel again, because this town will not let me leave its grasp, because I am born a woman into this century, borrowed into this caste, bound by cruel laws and cultural mores – because all of this restrains me, I will walk a pilgrimage in my mind.

And from the sacred bowl of my pelvis, I call to him.

And from the hallowed ground of my heart, I call to him.

And from the most esoteric secret of my consciousness, I call to him.

The god who loves us and gives us this life and these longings does so not so that we can refuse these gifts, but so that we can experience them, and in this way, give him joy that his creative delectations are not merely meant to be transcended, to be left behind.

And I do not stop pressing my stylus to palmyra leaves. Come what may, I do not stop telling the truth. I no longer only say the words under my breath as I write them down. I also stand before the altars, and I sing.

22

The bird in my throat is flightless. The bird in my throat is a bird of prey. *No.*

The bird in my throat is a parrot, that creature that listens intently and keeps no secrets. That mimics and memorizes. That serves as emissary for lovelorn women in cages. That perches on the finger of Meenakshi, parrot-green goddess of the city of Madurai and in northernmost Tamilagam on the shoulder of Kamakshi, the goddess whose eyes themselves are desire. That is the vehicle of the god who governs lust, Kamadeva. It is for him that I make something so beautiful that, for a moment, I long to keep it for myself.

I twist thin strands of banana stem fibre to form a skeleton, and cover this with tapioca leaves, padding layer upon layer so it thickens into form. At the bottom, I push sticks made from bamboo to form legs and talons, which I then wrap in the pink petals of oleander and moonbeam flowers. I spread feathers from palm fronds and place these as plumage for the wings and tail. I take a bright red pomegranate flower, halve it, and fold the beak from it. For the eyes, I affix a glittering stone known as crow's gold, the beads procured in the marketplace, where their seller told me they are found only in places where wells have been broken into the ground. And finally, I cut the slim peduncle that bears the heliconia flower, and encircle it delicately to make a rose-ringed neck. I am the daughter of a garland-maker, and for the lord of aphrodisia I have made with my hands a parrot, so as to hasten his work, so as to bring to me the one who will fill and fulfil me.

23

On many evenings, I walk to the Vatapatrasayi temple and stand forlorn before him for a while. This is not how the giver of his worn garland should be made to feel, ostracized and without remedy.

By now, the people of Puduvai have begun to call me Kodhai, the poet, and not just the poet's daughter. They know that I too have travelled to Madurai, and have been a guest of Raja Srimara Srivallabha. They must imagine I have spoken in the court, like my father, that I have bowed before the king himself and perhaps been given a token of appreciation that has been kept safely for my bride wealth.

They also see me, three times a day, offering flowers to the shrine of Kamadeva, painting secret diagrams on the sand, the same ones I draw on the walls of my innermost sanctum under the canopy of night. They hear me gather the winds with my incantations. I know I stand there as foolish as a peacock – splendour weighted and bound by its own plumage.

I spend less time on the stoop at the back of the house now, because for some reason seeing the cowherds now fills me with bitterness and shame. What was I playing at, to think I belonged to them, or that we were the same? I cannot have what they have, for they are free, and they cannot have what I have, because they are bound by the laws of caste. Animalar has become engaged. Uvakai and Eeranila are in no hurry, for they are still young in ways I am not sure I have ever been. They will find the ones they will love, or like Matatilli will find that there are many ways to love. Nothing suits me. I cannot bring Ayarpadi into the priestly quarters, no matter who birthed me or who the mother who raised me used to be. I cannot leave everything. It will not let me.

I ache.

I decide to visit them one evening, to walk from the temple through the familiar routes to the lake, where they must have returned by now. It is nearly nightfall, but I do not care. I want to see them in their own homes, in the landscape where we only so short a time ago prayed together like sisters. When I think of my dream of a thousand elephants now, I am filled with disgrace. Where were they, amidst those priestly rites and pots of gold? And my father, my mother? Padmamma with her feet so fragile she cannot even stand before God?

'Ay, rasathi!' Matatilli sights me as I take the last bend before her house. 'They have made you a princess, surely? Can we come with you and live in the palace?'

We embrace. Then she holds me at arms' length and frowns. 'What is happening to you?'

'I don't know.'

'Are you sick? Did someone hurt you? Why have you become so thin?'

'I am sad all the time,' I finally say. 'Praying and poetry change the fabric of my days, structure them, sweeten them. But this cannot be a whole life, can it? Why can it not be mine – a life of ordinary joys?'

Matatilli brushes away my tears and embraces me again. She says nothing at all.

A little later, I find Uvakai and Eeranila. We sit for a while in the wooden swing, held up with thick ropes, that hang under a huge peepal tree, taking turns. Their baby brother sleeps in a hammock made of one of their mother's saris nearby. The girls will be called home soon, as soon as their dinner is ready. Animalar is travelling with her parents. They have gone to some nearby town to buy her bridal trousseau.

When I go back home, Amma is in the kitchen preparing the night's meal, pounding red rice and coconut together to be steamed, and slicing yam to be fried. Something pungent with garlic boils on the stove. I ask her if I can help her. Instead of replying to me, and without turning back to look at me, she asks me a question.

'Who do you meet in the grove?'

'What do you mean?' I reply as evenly as I can.

'Who do you go to meet in the middle of the night, the one who makes you return in the morning smelling like wet earth?'

'No one.'

'You're lying.'

'It's true.'

My mother turns and looks at me for a long moment. 'When we were first married, your father and I would go into the grove at night.' Her eyes tell me what I should infer. 'It was difficult at first, with your grandparents…' She turns away and busies herself with stacking vessels. I gape at her back. And without turning to me again, she says, 'You are old enough to bring a man to this home now, but bring him here as my son-in-law. If you won't tell me who he is, you must stop meeting him before someone else sees what you are up to. Small towns have big eyes, you know this.'

'Amma—'

'Take this milk to Padmamma. Go now.'

I take the cup to my grandmother and stand before her dumbstruck until she finishes drinking it, for I do not know what else to do.

24

There is no man in any grove, in any forest, curtained behind the tents of some travelling circus, beyond the thunder of any waterfall – no man waiting for me. I would give anything for this to be true, for me to be like those girls who lie to their parents to spend afternoons in faraway fields with their hair spread on their lovers' chests. But no one has ever thought me worthy of too long a glance. If it was bad to be the poet's daughter, it is even worse now, to be the poet herself. A woman who can write herself to some other destiny, who can take flight on the passage of words.

There are no homes with rooms large enough for the wingspan of a woman like me, and so no one will ask me to enter his. Even in Madurai I had felt that: how I could move so freely because those were festival days, and only because I was counted among so many other foreigners.

So Kamadeva's grace is my target, and I intend to be the target of the arrow of his honey-drenched bow. And no matter where I am when it pierces me, my innermost eyes are always on my lord dark like conch vine flowers, whose own conch I envy for having known the taste of his coral lips. (Are they scented like camphor? Like lotuses?) Eye between the brows, eye between the thighs. Kamadeva's grace is like a lever with a beam and a fulcrum, or like a pair of weighing scales. There is always a counterpart. He will not leave me burning this way. The other half of my dyad will catch fire too, will blaze like sun-struck forest dryness. And he will come to quench me with his cool blue tulasi, his ocean-deep splendour, and he will overwhelm me. He will water me like rain. Vishnu himself, for in every story in which he has descended into this profane earth there is always a feminine grace who accompanies him, whom he must sometimes find or rescue. Or a man like Vishnu, but ephemerally human, dishevelled with passion, exalted by humility. No other will do.

25

I begin to fade. I begin to fray like the thatching on roofs after too many seasons. My moon blood becomes scant. I want to pluck these useless breasts of mine, untouched, and fling them at his own chest, and see then what he will see of me – blood and fire, worn down to bone, weakened to ash.

I am so lost, without direction. Through the month of Margali I worshipped Katyayani without fail in the biting cold. Through the months of Thai and Masi and now as Panguni dawns, I have worshipped Kamadeva three times a day, no matter where I have been, dropping my consciousness into the serene place from which I speak to him. And through my whole life I have adored that Krishna who marries me in my mirror every morning and by night ravishes me in the grove and in the great panorama of my imagination.

Not so far away is the month of Chithirai, and with it the new year and the intensifying heat of summer will be upon us. And we will be as far as we can be in the almanac from the brumal beauty of deep Margali.

And then a miracle happens.

Vishnuchittan wakes one morning carrying the smoky residue of a dream, and it spills from his mouth before he even goes to the well to bathe. He shakes us awake and says, 'The lord has called us. Kodhai will be wed to him in Tiruvarangam, where he reclines just as our Vatapatrasayi does, sleeping on the eternal ocean. He has come to me and asked for my daughter's hand, and I have accepted. Kodhai, we must prepare to leave. You are to be married. He has chosen you to be his bride.'

And so, this is how it will be. I will burn brightly awake and he will go on slumbering. Asleep on a banyan leaf, asleep on the endlessly coiling tail of the primordial serpent – but finally, and for eternity, asleep on the cradle of my breasts.

26

Katyayani Mahamayi Mahayogin Jathiswari Nandagopa Sudam Devi Pathim Me Kur De Namaha.

This is the secret verse that brings to the devout the thing that to them is love. You can have it, now that I have moved beyond the simple and certain. For no one should know the obscure and unlit places my heart has traversed in the absence of love. No one should be as deprived as I have been.

27

My last day in Puduvai dawns like any other. I rise from between my mother and grandmother and step out to the well to bathe and be ready for the garland that my father brings me, unable to hold back his tears. He is so proud to be the lord's new father-in-law, but to marry a daughter to anyone is also to lose her.

After this, I help my mother in the kitchen and pack a small meal for myself – fried gourd and foxtail millet mixed with just enough gravy that will not leak through the plantain leaf. And then I go to Shenbaga Thoppu.

In the marketplace, I manage to hitch a ride for part of the way. After that, I will only have to walk for a fraction of an hour to reach the coppice of magnolias.

It's a beautiful day of many breezes. Light clouds swirl above us in the bullock cart like bolls of cotton in these last days of Panguni. Once we are in the next calendar, a terrific storm will fill our reservoirs and wells just once before ushering in the greatest heat of the year, the time of the fire star. I have always enjoyed this season. Saplings take root with ease, and flowers bloom without needing to be coaxed. Nothing is too brittle or too thirsty to live.

Pollen kisses my cheeks and tickles my nostrils, and the winds carry with them the fragrances of many flowers, and mountain herbs, rich and with names that surpass my vocabulary.

I enter the coppice of magnolia trees, already in bloom, and some waft down to me, tailspun by the breeze, and adorn my open hair. I walk deeper and deeper in, and keep time with herds of small deer, observe the foreplay of langurs in heat, and even wade into a pond where bathing elephants cool themselves of the heat, and laugh as a calf – more playful than frightened – sprays me with her trunk.

And I lay by the waterfall and imagine myself a part of nature, ever changing yet unassailable. My hair curling like new sprigs on conch vine creepers. My breasts, ripe pomegranates. My radiant face the perigee moon. Between my thighs, a mollusc alive and made lambent by a pearl. I neither dream nor sleep, my eyes half-open like kinkini bells or night-blooming lilies by day. I simply breathe, and I never cease to be.

It is dusk when I re-enter Puduvai. I walk past the fields where cows and working people trudge through paths between the crops, tired, and past verdant orchards where fruits have just begun to ripen, colours blushing from the raw green like a parrot's beak from its face. And then I see that the small shrine to Kamadeva, listener to so many of my afternoon entreaties in a time before all this – before vows and journeys, before something in my heart began to wither then loosen like a leaf in the season of rains – is open. He is, of course, the one to whom I have made this most unequivocal of demands now. I wander in. There is hardly anyone here, and I bow before his idol and stare at him for a while. He who has no body, but has been cast in stone. The one whose vehicle is the parrot who listens carefully and betrays quickly, speaking to the world all the things whispered and moaned in secret, in the throes of love.

I have nothing more to ask. 'Kamadeva, you have given me nothing. And *he* has destroyed my womanhood,' I say. And then I walk away, my eyes burning.

There is a woman with a palmful of shells, a piece of cloth laid out before her, sitting just outside the compound of the shrine. She had ignored me as I entered, and still she does not raise her eyes to me. But I squat and greet her.

'Do you want me to look and tell you your fortune?' Her eyes are utterly exhausted.

'Yes.'

'What will you pay me?'

I think of that old story of Karnan, another child without lineage, who was the adopted son of a charioteer, and who did not know his origins until they were revealed to him as a gambit in a dirty war. Karnan's true father had been the sun, and because of this he was born with ornaments gleaming on his ears and armour on his chest. He was incapable of refusing any request. But he fought on the side that did not have God as its counsel, and one day a deity came to him in disguise and asked for his armour. He ripped it from his body and presented it without appeal – skin and blood on metal, raw wounds wind-bitten.

I slip one conch bangle off. It comes off without effort, for my limbs have thinned in these last few weeks from fasting and from heartsickness.

The woman accedes.

First she takes the conch bangle and places it beside her. Then she takes the shells in her palm, cowrie shells in the shape of a woman's mound. She blows on them, breathes words into them, and scatters them.

'There are three things,' she begins. 'The first is that naming alone cannot make a thing love. The second is that that which begins in fire must end in water. The third is that you will rule the world, you will rule all hearts, and you will always be the queen of jasmine country.'

My eyes pool with more tears. She too has given me nothing. I am left with one bare wrist and the bruise of having dared to hope, having still wanted something even after so much disintegration.

It's no use. I thank her and take my leave, and limp back to my house. It is in shadow as I approach, and I take a moment to look at it carefully, to imprint it in my heart, to thank it for having been my shelter through the sixteen and some years I have been on this earth. And then a small light moves into focus, reconfiguring the shadows. And she is standing there on the porch, a flame in her hand, in the pose I have seen all my life. My mother.

28

Amma and Padmamma weep freely as I leave Puduvai early the following morning, as the palanquin I sit on is lifted from the earth before our front porch. Four young men, all wearing the crossbelt, hold each end of the bamboo platform. They have made me wear my entire trousseau: gold and diamonds from my grandmother, pearls from my mother, and flowers from my father. My silk sari is red, shot through with gold threads that form borders of creeper vines and small, evenly spaced mango fruits along its length. The journey to Tiruvarangam will take seven days, and tonight when we stop to rest I must undress all this finery and wear it again only when we arrive. For the days and nights of the journey I will be weighed down by almost nothing – only the twin gems in my nose, cotton saris without thread-work, and a single conch bangle. My father will walk with my palanquin.

Dawn is barely breaking when we reach the Vatapatrasayi temple, where just outside the sanctum of Narasimha, my lion-man, another palanquin awaits. It shimmers and steals the eye with the ornaments that decorate it: light-snatching small mirrors, sparkling coins, tassels in many colours. The curtains are open. Within the palanquin is the most beautiful bronze sculpture I have ever seen. He is a processional idol, and his feet are not bonded within the cell of a sanctum. He stands proudly with his conch in one hand, his discus in another, a third hand in the gesture of blessing, and his fourth arm lowered, the hand concealed within wreaths of flowers, an embroidered shawl that drapes his shoulders, and the weight of his sparkling gem-studded necklace. He is Manavala Perumal, Vishnu the bridegroom. He too will accompany me to Tiruvarangam.

My palanquin is lowered so that I can pray at the temple, but first I stand before Manavala Perumal and take him in. How I wish I could lift him myself, to press him to my breasts and walk this journey with his metal body cooling my skin.

For seven days and as many nights we will travel, very slowly, to the city of Ranganatha, where the lord faces south, in the direction of Ilankai, a concession made to the one who had asked him to reside there. He had been on his way there when this small island ensconced between the rivers known as Kaveri and Kollidam had snagged his heart instead. So, he stayed and kept his eyes on Ilankai – where plumes of smoke still rose in the aftermath of Vishnu-Rama's war against Ravanan – and watched as tender green tendrils slowly began curling out from the earth, which grew to become forest cover, and as huts slowly rose, then citadels, and now the flag of the double fish in its far north.

There is music as we depart from the temple, and the performers follow the procession for a short distance. Even when they stop, they keep playing, so the sounds of the thavil and the nadaswaram fade slowly as we walk on. They are the last things I hear as I leave Puduvai for the final time.

My grandmother can barely walk, let alone travel, and so she binds my mother to her as granite binds spirit to stone. Wherever my mother came from, no matter how far she has wandered and what landscapes she holds within her heart-memory, it is in Puduvai that her life expends itself. She doesn't want me to leave as equally as she wants me to be free. When I clasped her for the last time, I almost couldn't let her go. But I did. Now, when we stop to rest along these highways, taking shelter in temples and on the thinnais of the rich who circle lit camphor before my face like I am Katyayani herself, I cry on some nights, wanting to hold Amma as I sleep, wanting so much the smell of coconut oil and firecracker flowers in her hair. So much that even if Krishna himself waited for me in the tulasi grove, in the bare and powerful body of a man, I would not lift my arm from around her so, so carefully, I would not slip my anklets from my feet and tiptoe through the door. I would not go.

But I am already gone.

What waits for me in Tiruvarangam? Once I have married the lord there is no guarantee that a mortal man will marry me, and even though I have rejected them all in principle, I have been on this earth not even seventeen years, and my waywardness has surely cursed my decades to come with loneliness.

What happens to the one who has seen the lord, merged with him, but also been allowed to continue to be a part of this world that is his play? It must be like descending from a mountaintop, bearing visions that lose their magic upon description. I have only heard stories of those who lived in constant god-drunkenness, and transformed into orbs of light when they perished, leaving no corpse. But this body of mine will not relent so quickly, will not turn into ether when it is so clearly made of woman-water, womb-fire, voice-wind and musk-mud.

Where is the century in which a woman like me can be free?

Where is a woman, like me, free?

29

When we travel, the palanquin bearers and my father bathe by wells. But Manavala Perumal and I bathe in temple tanks. In every town we pass, they allow us to rest, and often beg to have the honour of feeding us. People touch my feet with expressions of anguish as though I myself am a messenger bird, that mischievous parrot or that dulcet kuyil, as though I will arrive at my destination with their entreaties patterned like maruthani on my soles that so rarely touch the ground now.

When my moon blood comes, unexpected and out of order, I do not request that the journey be stopped. I tell them nothing. And they wouldn't even think of it. They believe I have risen above all that is bodily and mundane, let alone the body of a woman, lower than theirs in rank, with its odours and its ichors, its needs and its yielding. How little they know. How little they can even imagine.

How little they will ever know, those who only see what they want to see, who raise armies for what keeps them safe, but who do not see that these are the same things that keep them unable to be free.

30

Tonight, a full moon will rise over the gopurams of the city of Tiruvirangam, where the lord's temple is resplendent within the calyx of a tiny island.

We are but a few miles away, but hunger has overcome us, and so we have eaten at the home of a priest in a village just a little outside the city. And then, determined to go on, we continue – but the meal has made our eyelids heavy, and our stomachs bloated. The palanquins have been placed on the ground under the shade of a magnificent banyan tree, and each man has laid his head to rest. The river rustles just beyond, a low song that lulls the heart. There is nothing but quietness here, and the mellifluous chirps of black swallows and yellow-beaked mynas. I too lay on my back for a few minutes, gazing into the boughs of the tree, pondering its dense stranglers and its delicately shaped fig leaves, on which the lord I have loved all of my life sleeps and dreams, dreams and sleeps. I get up and walk over to his palanquin and part its curtains gently.

I lift him to my breasts, I take all his weight just as I longed for in those nights when I was sandalwood and earth, and longed to be somebody's, and I hold him so that his exquisite face is so close to mine that my breath touches him as I gaze into it. The strong incurvations of brow, the delicate strokes of his eyes, that finely carved nose and those lips – such lips – so perfectly hewn that they could be the twin petals of the cactus-kiss blossom.

O Ranganatha, O Manavala, you are mine at last.

The afternoon heat shimmers around me, the wind rippling the verdure on the river bank.

I loosen my sari and hold him inside it so that he is smothered right on my breasts, his cool metals quickening my heartbeat, electrifying me. And I bring the fabric's loose end around me tightly so that he is tied to me, and then I embrace him just as I have always dreamed of doing.

And then I walk into the water and let the Kaveri glide over us. My heart is incandescent as she sweeps us completely into her embrace. And then, we are a part of her, riverine and absorbed deeply. Immersed.

AUTHOR'S NOTE

'She asked the lovely conch with its spirals about
Mayan's red lips.
She is the queen of the Malli Nadu.
She is the wild parrot
who adorned her lovely hair with a garland
meant for the lord of Arangam.
We find refuge in her pure and virtuous feet.'

—An anonymous taniyan prefixed to the *Nachiyar Tirumoli*

translated from the Tamil by Archana Venkatesan

Each year in the Tamil month of Margali, which corresponds with the Gregorian period of mid-December to mid-January, Vaishnavite temples in Tamil Nadu resound with the recitation of the *Tiruppavai*, thirty verses in the voice of a young cowherd woman supplicating the god Vishnu to give her a mysterious drum, bring abundant prosperity to her land and to bless her and her troupe of friends for their worship. These verses describe the rituals of the pavai nombu, presumably observed by young women of medieval India who sought a fine husband, and are also described by the *Bhagavata Puranam*. The *Tiruppavai* is attributed to the poet Andal, who in her lifetime was named Kodhai, a word that means 'garland'. If the poet's other work, the *Nachiyar Tirumoli*, is recited at all, the anonymous taniyan (laudatory verse) that precedes it is usually omitted. The *Nachiyar Tirumoli* itself – almost in its entirety, with the exception of 'Vaaranam Aayiram', the dream of a thousand elephants, which is sung at weddings – is often alluded to, but as often elided. Beginning exactly where the girlish, joyous *Tiruppavai* ends, it makes a dramatic shift – the poet's voice turns despairing, her demands and preoccupations visceral and openly sensual.

I have wondered who wrote that taniyan, whose name too is lost but whose words, despite omission, have not been expurgated. It is only one of many things we will never know about the life and work of Kodhai who became Andal. As Andal, she is canonized as one of the twelve Alvars – devotional poets whose verses praised, questioned and adored Vishnu. The word 'alvar' means 'one who is immersed'.

The traditional story of Andal is as follows: she was a divine incarnation discovered in a tulasi grove tended by Periyalvar, a poet of the priestly caste who had the patronage of the Pandya king Srimara Srivallabha of Madurai, who chose to raise her (canonical tellings do not mention a mother, but I have heard of unusual ones that do). As a child, she would steal and wear the garland her father made for Vishnu. When she was caught and reprimanded, the deity refused to accept any garland that was not first worn by Andal. As she grew up, she fell more and more deeply in love with Vishnu, and when she was taken to the Tiruvirangam temple (present day Srirangam, Tamil Nadu) to be married to him, she disappeared into the idol of Vishnu-Ranganatha in a flash of light. Like her father, Andal too was a poet. In an honour not accorded to other Alvars, she is considered a goddess, and as the only woman among the twelve who ascends into divinity through marriage to the divine. A temple in Srivilliputhur (believed to be modern-day Puduvai), seventy kilometres south of Madurai, is the main site of her worship.

Kodhai's epithet, Andal, means 'she who rules'. Other poets who appear in these pages, who are now known by other names, are Vishnuchittan (Periyalvar), Satagopan (Nammalvar) and Vadhavoorar (Manickavasagar). Periyalvar and Nammalvar, as their names indicate, were also among the Vaishnavite Alvar canon. Manickavasagar belongs to the Saivite Nayanmar canon of sixty-three poets who sang in praise of Shiva. His *Tiruvempavai*, like Andal's *Tiruppavai*, is sung in the month of Margali and alludes to the pavai nombu. Each pasuram (or verse) in both these works ends on the same mysterious refrain: *el or empavaay*.

In any work of historical fiction, an author must make choices that are partly intuitive, even if debatable. For example: would Andal have known of the *Silapathikaram*,

Ilango Adigal's Tamil epic set in Madurai and dated to as early as 3CE? Very likely, for there are certain motifs in both Andal's work and Ilango's that suggest it, and the dance that takes place in Madurai in this book is inspired by it. But the Kodhai who came to me didn't. She found Nappinai not in literature but in the form of a woman she knew and loved.

Andal remains exalted and worshipped, if not cherished, to this day. But who was Kodhai? I did not rely on intuition alone to fill the lacuna, the misalignment, between her poetry and her popular hagiography. What made my understanding of Kodhai possible were the many ways in which this hagiography itself changes upon repetition, or based on the storyteller. Of these, of particular meaning were: an informal lecture in 2016 by Pradeep Chakravarthy in which the detail of a processional idol of Manavala Perumal being carried alongside Andal's palanquin to Srirangam made the novel's culmination appear before me; what I read second hand of the various elaborations of the 12CE *Divyasuricharitram* of Garuda Vahana Panditha; and Priya Sarukkai Chabria's short story 'Why I Am Called Periyalvar and How My Daughter Became a Goddess'. In the scene with 'the ceremony of flowers', I connected the poochoodal function in Sarukkai Chabria's story to verses of Periyalvar's known by the same name, in which the baby Krishna is coaxed to wear different blossoms his mother has collected. The verses of Satagopan's that Vishnuchittan recites in Srimara Srivallabha's court are taken from A.K. Ramanujan's translation, *Hymns for the Drowning*. The lines that end the first chapter reference a poem attributed to Kaccipettu Nannakaiyar from the *Kuruntokai*, a collection of love poetry dating to the Sangam era. And of course, throughout my text are allusions to Andal's own poetry.

Andal belongs to a pantheon from which she will never be shaken. But who was Kodhai, the teenager in a small town in ninth-century Tamil Nadu, filled with yearnings that she sublimated into poetry? In her poems are all the desires and disappointments of a wholly human nature. In this imperfect and temporal locus was where I found her at her most sublime.

Sharanya Manivannan
Vaikasi/June 2018

SELECT BIBLIOGRAPHY

Chabria, Priya Sarukkai and Shankar, Ravi, *Andal: The Autobiography of a Goddess*, New Delhi: Zubaan Books, 2016

Dehejia, Vidya, *Antal and Her Path of Love: Poems of a Woman Saint from South India*, New York: State University of New York Press, 1990

Devnath, Lakshmi, *Poorva: Magic, Miracles & The Mystical Twelve*, Chennai: Notion Press, 2016

Krishnadevaraya (trans. Srinivas Reddy), *The Giver of the Worn Garland: Krishnadevaraya's Amuktamalyada*, New Delhi: Penguin India, 2011

Nammalvar (trans. A.K. Ramanujan), *Hymns for the Drowning*, New Delhi: Penguin India, 2005

Venkatesan, Archana, *The Secret Garland: Andal's Tiruppavai and Nacciyar Tirumoli*, New Delhi: Harper Perennial, 2016

Venkatesan, Archana, Branfoot, Crispin and Arni, Clare, *In Andal's Garden: Art, Ornament and Devotion in Srivilliputtur* Mumbai: The MARG Foundation, 2015

ACKNOWLEDGEMENTS

Thank you to Shiamila Komahan and Taarun, who wandered with me through the places Kodhai knew.

To my editor, Sohini Basak, whose keen eye always sees more of what can be.

To Dr Archana Venkatesan, both for the grace and beauty of her translations of and scholarship on the Alvars and for the generosity with which she responded to my queries.

I cannot forget the first time I heard Priya Sarukkai Chabria's multivalent translations of Andal's poetry in Chennai in late 2011. I am especially grateful for her short story 'Why I Am Called Periyalvar and How My Daughter Became a Goddess' (from *Andal: The Autobiography of a Goddess*).

I wish the late Dr Dennis Hudson could know how vital his paper *Tantric Rites in Antal's Poetry* (from *Tantra in Practice*, edited by David White) was to my seeing Kodhai. His scholarship transformed my wondering to wonderment, giving me a perfect explanation for the shift in tone between the *Tiruppavai* and the *Nachiyar Tirumoli*. His paper *Pinnai, Krishna's Cowherd Wife* (from *Radha and the Goddesses of India*, eds. John Stratton Hawley and Donna Marie Wulff) was also especially illustrative.

The description of the parrot that Kodhai makes as an offering to Kamadeva owes much to an article in *The Hindu* ('Labour of Love', 8 August 2013) on S. Raman, the Srivilliputhur temple's hereditary parrot-maker.

To everyone, known and unknown, who made possible my encounters with Andal – in Tamil, in English, and in the absence of words. Whose voices brought me her verses in song, whose pamphlets and books I read them in, whose paintings she smiled at me from. Thank you.

My deepest gratitude is to the one who sang in me, the poet who came to me as muse.

ALSO BY SHARANYA MANIVANNAN

'Sharanya's poems are, in her own phrase, a form of phosphorescence – glowing in darkness, simmering with wonder, mythic in resonance, boldly embodied, hence surprisingly spiritful, even spiritual in the finest sense of the word. They are also sceptical and reflective, tempering and enhancing the glowing flame. Riptides of Tamil hide beneath or within her honed English, for those who can hear and see.'

– David Shulman

ALSO BY SHARANYA MANIVANNAN

'Strung like luminous pearls, *The High Priestess Never Marries* is a collection of evocatively written short stories that feature women who seem suspended between relationships, living in moments fraught with desire and despair. Set in current day Chennai, these unnamed female protagonists cherish their independence, even within the bounds of relationships, and find their inner voices through an exploration of sensuality and choice. These are women who have accepted their many loves, their imperfect selves, and their fractured lives.'

– South Asia Laadli Media and Advertising Award for Gender Sensitivity 2015-2016 (Best Book - Fiction)

Photograph by Jaison G